BULLETPROOF

ORIGINS

STEPHEN J. MITCHELL

Cover Illustration
Copyright © 2019 Matt Flint

Cover design: Donna Refici

Author photograph
Copyright © 2019 Vanessa Deaton Photography

Paperback Edition: September 2020

Copyright © 2019 Stephen J. Mitchell
Critical Blast Publishing
All rights reserved.
ISBN: 978-0-578-75108-5

DEDICATION

For Damion, Dakotah, and Sarissa.

With you in my life…

…I feel bulletproof.

PROLOGUE

Looking over his research, Doctor Eric Haywood was frustrated with the slow rate of development his experiment showed. He had been working on a scaled down version and, according to his findings, the maturity rate for the serum was approximately eighteen years. Even though he sped up the process once already, this would not make his benefactor happy. Millions of dollars for his research had been invested, and there was no way he could justify getting more.

Although he had, and multiple times. But the Khan was getting very suspicious, so he dared not to do it again.

For the first time in his life he was stumped. Well, the second really. It wasn't until his third semester at Johns

Hopkins University that he fell in love with one of his lab partners, Sumiko. A student of biophysics, he had never encountered a challenge more difficult than decoding a woman's emotions. She was hesitant at first, as she was originally from Japan and planned on returning home to care for her grandfather after she got her degree. But Eric's perseverance paid off, and they were married soon after graduation.

For Eric, every challenge came with a prize. And since there was no consolation in losing, he never quit on anything. It was a strength of his, as much as it was a weakness.

In this moment, he was about ready to quit. But there was too much at stake. He took off his glasses and rubbed at his eyes. Between his notes, the computer monitor, and the vials of serum on his desk, it was all proving to be more frustrating than productive. He stared at the same information, hoping something would magically change by looking away and then back again.

It wasn't working.

As revolutionary as his research would be, no one would want to wait years for the mutation to fully evolve. The subject would be well past their prime. There was only one way to make it worthwhile, but to even suggest it would have him vilified in any scientific community. If not for Sue's efforts to protect the inhumane treatment of animals, he would've ordered tests on live subjects long ago. He saw that as proof that he loved her more than his work.

Eric's longtime friend and partner, Nathan Powell, sat down at a nearby desk holding freshly printed data in his hand. Eric never understood why Nathan worked such late nights to assist him. He was a handsome bachelor and could easily be out playing doctor rather than actually being one. Whenever they attended a convention together, Nate's dimpled smile and light-blue eyes had colleagues of all types wanting to run their fingers through his blonde hair.

Even though Nate hadn't accomplished much

scientifically, he was a celebrity on his looks alone. The man was a work of art.

"Still nothing?" Nate asked.

Eric leaned back in his chair and stared at the disorganized mess of documents, charts and books opened before him. "No," he replied. "This is getting frustrating. I feel like we're so close to an answer. I'm confident that once we perfect this, the government will give us the funding we need to mass produce the serum. And, maybe, provide us amnesty from our current benefactor."

"You mean if they don't brand us as traitors and have us executed?" Nate said half-jokingly. "Because you know that's in play once they discover we've been working with terrorists," he added with a more serious tone.

"Always the optimist, my friend," Eric replied with exhaustion.

A noise in the hallway startled the two men and caused them to freeze. Holding their breath, they looked at each other in silence. After a moment, they cautiously went back to work, frequently looking up at the door to the lab. At 2 in the morning, it's wasn't likely to be anyone but housekeeping. Still, Eric was paranoid.

Not even Sue knew that he was working in the lab.

Then, something on the monitor caught Eric's eye. It was as though he was seeing it for the first time and the formulas shifted around in his mind. He rubbed his eyes under his glasses, cursing his fatigue for not being able to focus on the data that danced before him. He blinked a couple of times and then he saw it. There was the code that could speed up the process! He tapped away at his keyboard, in a frenzy, and once he made the proper adjustments to the formula, he was ready to build the serum.

At Eric's request, Nathan prepped the chemicals.

Eric smiled. It would be a one in a million chance for the body to nurture the serum on its own, because of its tendency to create antibodies. This would drastically reduce the number of soldiers it would work on, but it wouldn't matter. In the end, they would be unstoppable.

Another hour passed before Eric and Nathan had several vials of serum. The dark green liquid looked putrid, almost swampy in color, as though he threw muck and seaweed in a blender. With a frown, Eric inserted one vial into the back end of a syringe while Nathan rolled up his sleeve.

"You sure you want to do this?" Eric asked.

"All I can say is I'm extremely happy I don't have to drink it." Nathan flashed a dimpled smile and held his arm out.

A loud banging on the door interrupted them.

Eric paused for a moment and held his breath. Nathan had a look of fear in his eyes, as though someone was holding a gun to his head.

"Doctor Haywood, we know you're in there!" The voice had a thick Middle Eastern accent. "More importantly, we know you have been keeping the research from us!"

Another knock at the door. "Doctor, it is not wise to steal money from the Khan!"

The clicking of guns in the hallway kick-started Eric's adrenaline. His heart pounded against his chest. It didn't matter what he did or where he went now. They had found him, and his entire operation had been exposed.

He was a dead man.

Grabbing the mouse, he steadied his hand. With several clicks he downloaded files onto a flash drive. Moving the pointer over a file on his desktop labeled *Hide and Seek*, he opened it and immediately the screen turned into a jumbled mix of zeroes and ones. Binary code flashed on the screen.

A methodic, loud banging against the door told him they were trying to break it down. It was a reinforced frame, so Eric knew he had a few moments to spare. He looked up to see Nate frantically unplug his computer and grab the documents on his desk; shoving them into an open briefcase on the floor.

He needed to buy some time. He ran over to the north

wall and pulled the fire alarm. A loud siren blared, as the room went dark and emergency lights flashed.

"Eric, hurry up, we need to get out of here!" Nathan barred the door shut by sliding a desk in front of it. It wouldn't hold the Khan's men for long, but it was enough to give them a head start on their escape.

Without looking, Eric reached up and grabbed the syringe off the desk and set it into a pocket of the briefcase. He closed the lid and latched it tight.

Out in the hallway, gunshots were fired.

Eric clutched the briefcase to his chest. Looking to the emergency exit on the other side of the lab he ran to it. Nate quickly followed. The door opened enough for the Khan's men to squeeze through. As they entered one by one, the terrorists opened fire, spraying bullets around the room with reckless abandon. Papers flew off of desks and computers sparked as a relentless volley of ammunition ripped through the lab. Eric leapt over a desk as if he were back on the high school football team. Nathan stumbled over a chair, but he quickly regained his balance and kept moving.

When they reached the emergency exit, a bullet struck Eric's left shoulder, spinning him around and sending him to the floor.

"Eric!" Nathan stopped and dove to the floor next to him. The guns continued to fire as he crawled over to help his friend.

"Take the briefcase." Eric tried to give it to Nathan, who quickly rejected it.

"No way, man! I'm not getting caught with that. Now get up and get moving, so I don't have to die too."

Eric nodded in agreement.

The gunfire stopped while their attackers reloaded. Reaching up, Nate opened the door and pulled Eric out with him. The door slammed shut and they both took a deep breath as bullets thumped against the heavy door.

Standing up with his friend's help, Eric grit his teeth. He had never been shot before and wasn't looking forward to it happening again. Knowing the heavy security door would keep the Khan's men at bay, he motioned to the staircase going down.

A few moments later, Nate was helping Eric into his car. "You're bleeding everywhere. We need to get you to a hospital."

"No!" Eric protested. "You remember the contingency plan, right? It's time. No matter what happens…stick to the plan," he said through gritted teeth.

"I know, stick to the plan," Nathan said as his eyes cut to the briefcase. "Do what you have to do, and we'll meet up at the rendezvous point." Nathan shut the door and rested his fist against the window. Eric reached up and pressed his fist against it as well, flinching at the pain in his shoulder.

He watched as his friend got into his own car and drove off. Eric's vision began to blur and everything went black.

Years ago, Eric had made a shrewd business deal with a billionaire to do research on a genome project that would benefit all mankind. Accused of attempting to play God, he had been denied a patent and grant from the US government. Months later, he had been contacted by a benefactor with an offer he couldn't refuse. In exchange for the completed product, he would be given unlimited funds to complete his research. Blinded by the euphoria from finally having someone to back his research, he didn't realize he was dealing with a radical terrorist group headed by a man only known as 'The Khan.' It was only when they paid him a visit, to check on his progress, that he pieced it together.

They left him bloodied and beaten in his lab. When Sumiko found out, she threatened to pack up their son, Dan, and leave him unless he cut ties immediately. Promising he would turn over his research, he used the money to move their family to a safer location. As a show of good faith, he even brought Sue's father over from Japan to keep him nearby.

But he couldn't let go of his dream so easily.

Moving the family to Port Haven, he looked up his old friend, Nathan Powell, a professor at the local university, and brought him on as a silent partner. Secretly skimming money off the top of what The Khan sent him, Eric set up separate nest eggs for his wife and kids in case anything happened. Knowing Khan wanted to remain anonymous, he was certain the money they had given him was untraceable. That put millions of unmarked dollars into his hands, which was easily hidden from their view in return.

Things began growing heated as the Khan grew more impatient with the lack of progress. Threats were made. When an 'accident' put Sue in the hospital, he realized they had found his family and his time was limited. Realizing his family was in constant danger, he devised a contingency plan.

Now The Khan had sent his men to kill him, and he was on the run.

Turning off his headlights, he pulled into the driveway and shut off the engine. Eric didn't remember the drive home. Shaking off the thought, he knew he had to keep moving. Grabbing his briefcase, he slipped quietly through the back door, making sure he left it open a crack. This would be a short visit.

It would be his last one.

Eric checked on his oldest son, Daniel. At ten years old, he was quite the athlete. Strong. Healthy. He was sad that he wouldn't be able to watch him compete anymore. Eric didn't have a lot of time for his family but he enjoyed playing catch with his oldest son when he could. Dan had a great arm. Hopefully Sue would keep him in sports.

Eric went to his bedroom, where Sumiko was sleeping. He gave her a kiss on the forehead; a gentle one so as not to wake her. He left a note on her nightstand, a note he had written the night their infant son, Kody, was born. It said how sorry he was for betraying her, and for not being the man she believed him to be.

Then he moved into the nursery.

Little Kody lay in his crib, peacefully sleeping on his side. That was rather unusual, as Sumiko would tell him that his son was a restless sleeper. Watching his son, he forgot about all of his worries, if only for a brief moment. When Kody flinched, Eric caught his breath praying that he didn't wake up. Instead he only shifted a bit and made a suckling noise. Eric smiled. How could he have missed out on moments like these with Dan? How could he have thrown away the chance to experience the joy of raising a child the second time around?

The answer made what he was about to do that much more difficult.

Setting his briefcase on the changing table, he popped the latches and opened it. Eric pulled out the syringe and held it up to the window, where the moon offered the only light in the room. Tapping it a few times to make sure there were no pockets of air, he winced. He wondered why his shoulder hurt so much. That's when he remembered he had been shot. The loss of blood was making him delusional.

He had to move faster.

Leaning in to the crib, he whispered into his son's ear. "Forgive me." He took a deep breath and held it, to steady his hands. With one swift motion he inserted the needle into the thick part of his son's thigh, injected the serum and slid the needle out.

Kody screamed in pain, his sleep interrupted by the prick of the needle. Eric tried to push himself away from the crib but the room spun and he fell against the changing table instead. Gathering himself up, he pulled a box out of the closet and placed his briefcase inside.

"What's going on?"

Sumiko.

Eric turned so quickly he nearly passed out; he didn't have much time left. His wife entered the room and picked up the baby to console him.

"Sue, I-I need to go," Eric forced out. "They found us.

You need to move far away from here. I will keep them away for as long as I can."

"Oh Eric," she said, beginning to cry. "Why? I thought you were done with this. You *told* me you were done with this!"

"I'm sorry, I-I..." His words trailed off. He planned everything down to hiding his family, but he didn't prepare an apology for his wife. The woman he loved since the day they met. He pulled an envelope stuffed with money and handed it to her. "Use this to pay for the move. Hide the kids, hide yourself. I'll contact you as soon as it's safe."

Sumiko held Kody in her arms and took the envelope. Words escaped her. She watched as her bleeding and disillusioned husband used all of his power to hide a box in the closet. When he was done, he looked to her for a hug. She turned her back on him and moved to the rocking chair, fighting back her own tears to help her son overcome his.

"Sumiko I-"

"Get out!" she said in a forced whisper, hoping not to wake Daniel, or her father who lived in the guest room downstairs. "I won't have this house raided because you broke your promise to me. If you're going to go...then go." Her words came out through tears and gritted teeth, as though she wanted to cry and scream, but restrained herself for the sake of the sleeping household.

Eric didn't remember how he got into his car; only that he was there and his hands were on the keys. Why hadn't he started the car? What was he doing at his house? Everything was going smoothly; he couldn't be caught here. There was something he needed to do, but since he couldn't remember, he moved on to the next phase of his plan: get out of town and disappear.

Each day that had passed had brought Eric closer to the realization that developing a successful serum may not happen. His thesis was convincing enough. Enough for the Khan to invest in his project when his own country's top military minds laughed him out of the Pentagon. The

Khan's investment meant success or death—to Eric and anyone he cared about. If he succeeded, he would return to the Pentagon and give them a chance to outbid the Khan. It was a risky grift, to be sure, but he was a gambling man. And he could protect his family—a family The Khan didn't even know about at the time. He took great care in making sure that, if he failed, they would not suffer for his sins. He selected a random family several miles from his own; a single mother raising two children. He did what was necessary to throw the Khan off the scent of his real family. Their lives meant nothing to him other than shielding the ones he loved. The Khan's men could do with them as they pleased.

His failure had meant they would die. Innocent people, with no clue why they would be butchered. Even still, he had one more contingency up his sleeve. A fake serum. The Khan would receive it, and, by the time his deception was discovered, Eric would already be several steps ahead.

Unfortunately, even with his contingencies, it had all fallen apart. He had no choice but to run and hide. While his life may be close to over, he had to buy his family time. The longer they hunted him, and the longer the breadcrumb trail he left behind, the less likely that The Khan would discover his actual family. He would use himself as bait for as long as he could to keep them busy.

Now the rats were out of their cage, looking for cheese on the move. For a moment he thought about the decoy family, but he quickly pushed them out of his mind. He refused to allow himself to get sentimental about people he didn't know.

It was now all about keeping his family safe. No matter the cost.

It was all he could do to make it up to them.

He hoped that someday he would be able to face his family, and that they would understand why he did it. There were so many things he would miss out on because of the bad decisions he made. He had widowed his wife, orphaned his children.

Someday though, maybe...just maybe, he could tell them a story with a happy ending.

STEPHEN J MITCHELL

Today...

Kody Haywood ran as though his life depended on it.

Things never seemed to work out the way he planned. It seemed everywhere he went, someone was chasing him. Without warning, he became the focus of everyone's attention. And while he normally didn't mind, he was out of his element here.

He had the one thing his pursuers wanted, and they would stop at nothing to bring him down. People were relying on him, and that didn't happen often; he had a reputation for being forgetful, unfocused, and undisciplined. No matter how hard he tried to do the right thing, it always seemed to blow up in his face.

With three people left chasing him, he was only thirty yards away from reaching his goal. His chest heaved, as he gasped for air. His legs burned as he ran. Despite the discomfort, he pressed on, refusing to be caught. Looking over his shoulder, he realized he was on his own now.

He wasn't about to drop the ball; not when he was so close.

Sweat dripped down his brow and stung his eyes. For a moment, he considered surrendering himself. But the thought of what they'd do if they caught him caused adrenaline to surge through his body. Fear gave him the boost he needed to leap in the air with his arms outstretched.

As he hit the ground, a high-pitched noise pierced his eardrums.

"Touchdown, blue team!" The gym teacher, Mr. Maris, made a note on his clipboard while chewing his whistle.

Kody tried to stand, and was shoved back down, his face hitting the ground hard. The blades of grass pricked at his cheek. It smelled freshly cut, and carried a hint of gasoline from the lawnmower used by the school groundskeeper.

An elbow pressed into his back. A knee slammed into his ribs. Three kids decided to take their anger out on him for scoring.

"You should have just let us tackle you," Jared said.

"Yeah what's the point in trying to score? It's just gym class you idiot." Paul added.

Kody grunted his reply, "In that case, I should try out for the team to make things a little more interesting."

He struggled to get up but their combined weight was too much for him to even move.

"Don't even think about it, loser," Brett said. "We want winners playing for the Bucs." Brett Walker was Bannerville High School's most popular student and captain of the football team.

Kody thought of him as the one everybody loved to hate, but nobody would ever say it to his face. There was an edge to Brett, and he always seemed to be on it. There wasn't a single kid in school who would think about crossing him for fear of getting beat up. Kody, however, wasn't often accused of thinking.

Bannerville High was the biggest school in Port Haven which meant it attracted scouts from all of the biggest colleges. Brett was the school's biggest prospect since Kody's older brother, Dan, had graduated six years prior. This made Brett a really big deal, and made Kody the butt of jokes as he lived in his brother's academic and athletic shadow.

Brett was starting quarterback for the Bannerville Bucs. He was the best player on the team, and loved to brag about it. He was also the school's biggest jerk, as if being team captain was a free pass to get away with murder.

Brett could do no wrong.

"Yeah," Paul added. "We want winners."

Kody tried to look up with just his eyes, as his cheek was still pressed to the turf. "Do you just repeat whatever Brett says? Are you his parrot?" Then in his best pirate voice, he added, "*Do ya get ta ride on the captain's shoulder?*"

"Don't answer that Paul."

"Yeah, I don't have to answer that," Paul replied.

Kody smiled. "*Paulie want a cracker?*"

The boy answered with a kick to the ribs. Surprisingly, it didn't hurt. It should have. Paul was big for his age; some kids said that what he lacked in brains he made up for in brawn. He was Bannerville's starting Defensive Tackle, and if 'human tractor' was a job, Kody figured Paul could be employee of the month someday.

"Hey!" Mr. Maris shouted from across the field. "You boys quit horsin' around! You wanna get hurt? The only first aid I administer is 'walking it off' and 'rub some dirt on it!' Now get off your butts and get back in the huddle!"

Jared and Paul got off of Kody, but Brett knelt down next to him. "You better tell Coach Maris you're hurt so you can sit out during the next play." He looked back at Mr.

Maris, who was preoccupied with a few other kids. Leaning in closer he added, "Otherwise, I'm gonna hurt you for real. I don't care who your brother was, you're not trying out for the team. You're a loser, and you'll always be a loser."

"Am I a loveable loser?" Kody said sarcastically.

"More like laughable loser, and you'll never be the hero to this school that I am."

A bell rang loudly, signaling the end of class.

"Literally saved by the bell," Kody muttered under his breath.

Mr. Maris hollered, "Alright everyone, get changed and get to your next class! There's learnin' to be done and I'm not here to teach!"

"See ya, loser." Brett stepped on Kody's leg as he and his friends headed back inside.

"Love that energy!" Kody gave two thumbs up to the boys as they walked away. "We should really do this more often. So much fun."

A couple of girls walked by him. When they made eye contact, he smiled. They laughed among themselves and kept walking.

Kody pulled himself to his feet and brushed some of the dirt off his clothes. He inspected a tear in his shirt, but couldn't remember if it was bought that way from the thrift store.

He hated the torment he dealt with each day. No matter where he was, trouble seemed to find him. Getting picked on was a typical day of school for him. Whether it was his clothes, his personality, or even his long, shaggy, black hair, kids always found something to tease him about.

There were some days he wanted to just hit someone, but he refused to do it. That wasn't heroic behavior. And he looked up to heroes, whether they were in comic books or in real life. He loved reading about their deeds. He wanted to be one someday. He wanted to hear a crowd of people cheering him on.

Ever since Kody reached the 9th grade, there had been

a lot of pressure on him to be the next hero of Bannerville High School. His teachers always talked about how someday he would be 'the next big quarterback and team captain of Bannerville High.' His older brother, Dan, was a celebrity for bringing the Bannerville Bucs their only state championship six years ago, and everyone thought he would be the next one to do it. Until Brett came along.

But Kody's grades were so poor, he couldn't play sports if he wanted to. Which he didn't.

Kody didn't like sports or the pressure that came along with them. He could go from hero to zero just from having one bad game. He wanted more control over his fate than that. Instead, he preferred spending his days reading comic books, playing video games, skateboarding, and training under Shihan Toshihiro's guidance in the art of Aikido.

Aikido was a defensive style of martial arts that uses an opponent's momentum against themselves. It was one of Kody's favorite things to practice.

It helped him maintain focus.

If there was one thing in particular that he struggled with the most, it was paying attention. His mind often wandered off in different directions, getting him lost in his own thoughts. Sometimes he would lose focus and find himself staring off at nothing, his mind racing with a thousand thoughts all at once.

He wished there was a way to stop it.

There were many times people accused him of ignoring them, but that wasn't the case. He just couldn't pay attention as a conversation dragged on. Which meant, while a teacher was teaching, Kody eventually drifted off and didn't hear most of the lesson. He was grateful he had smart friends who took notes and kept him on track.

His best friend in the whole world was Gene Franklin. Gene was a prodigy, a genius who had been fast-tracked to high school because the middle grades weren't challenging enough for him. Demonstrating a maturity well beyond his years, Gene's parents left him home alone frequently as they spent most of their time on business trips. He had his own credit card, so he could take care of any expenses he had.

For being only twelve years old, Gene was even smart with his money. Kody couldn't understand how the boy genius was just naturally good at knowing things. It was like his brain was a computer, and his parents just uploaded all the information he needed.

Kody's other friend, Caliente Cruz, 'Callie' for short, was Brazilian and had only been in America for a few years. After her mother died, she moved to Port Haven with her father, who got a job working the docks. The two of them became friends when Kody saw her being harassed by a group of kids, and he had stepped in to make them stop.

He took a beating, but it worked. He always took a beating, it seemed. And today's gym class was no exception.

The bell rang for the second time, and Kody looked around.

He stood in front of his locker on the second floor of Bannerville High School. The hallway was empty. Slamming his locker shut, he cursed under his breath. His mind had wandered again. He had no clue how he got there or how long he'd been there. Checking his schedule, he realized it was his lunch period.

He gave the combination lock a spin and headed down to the first-floor cafeteria, where his friend Gene would be waiting in the same place he always did: the broken table. It was a reject among all of the other tables, as it had a wobbly leg and a crack down the middle of it. Tucked away in the corner, nobody else sat there.

Kody met Gene for the first time when he saw him sitting at the table. Being the youngest student in high school by several years, Gene often felt like an outcast. So he found himself sitting at the table no one else would. Gene said the table was more welcoming to him than any of the kids in the cafeteria were. When Kody saw him there all alone, he couldn't help but to sit down and start talking to him. Kody knew what it was like to feel the way Gene did, having grown up poor and without parents.

Because Kody wore tattered clothes and everything was generic, he was often teased. On top of that, he was being raised by an old Japanese man who ran an Aikido school. He didn't know how that old man had become his foster parent, but it was all he knew so he never questioned it.

Although Kody had an older sibling, Dan, he never saw him or talked with him. As much as he hated school, there were days when he felt more alone at home, like an outcast, lacking a full family.

The first day they met, Kody sat down next to Gene and asked the smaller, younger, boy if he was lost. Gene was impressed by the fact that Kody wasn't at all intimidated by his intelligence. Whether it was because Kody was just a good person, or because he didn't pay attention, didn't matter to him. Gene was just grateful that someone wasn't afraid to be seen with the short, dark-skinned, pre-teen with an IQ that would make scholar's jealous.

There were times when Gene thought people were more intimidated by his IQ than his skin color. But not Kody. Kody Haywood didn't pay attention to either of those things. Gene deduced that his quick-witted, aloof, shaggy-haired, friend was more interested in just enjoying life, regardless of his own situation.

Gene wondered what it must be like to be so carefree.

After Kody got his tray of food, he sat down where he always did, next to Gene, being sure to avoid the split where the table was falling apart. Knowing his luck, today would be the day it gave out and crashed to the floor.

"You're late," Gene said. "Did you get lost in your head again?"

"Yeah," Kody replied, looking at his food as though he wasn't sure how it got there. "But hey, at least I didn't have to wait in line! How's your day so far?"

"Quite intriguing to say the least," Gene replied, pushing his glasses up. "My physics instructor attempted to disallow my theory of reverse gravitational thrust containment. I did not concur with what I believed to be his illogical conclusions, and insisted that he review my full thesis."

"Wow," Kody replied, extremely confused. "Gravitational something-or-whatnot, huh? Well, don't let him discourage you. He's probably just jealous that you know more about gravity than the cookie guy."

"The 'cookie' guy?" Gene raised an eyebrow.

"Yeah, Newton."

"Are you implying that Sir Isaac Newton, who theorized gravity, is also responsible for giving us cookies filled with fig?"

"Yeah, that's him. The cookie guy."

"Kody, he did not invent the cookie."

"Sucks to be him, because those are some good cookies. Plus, if I eat enough of them, gravity takes over, if you catch my meaning." Kody made a fart sound with his mouth.

"Gross. Anyway," Gene carried on with his original point, "Mr. Jennings said he does not have time to read my thesis. I say he is trying to avoid feeling inferior."

"What's that supposed to mean?" Kody wondered.

"He's clearly racist."

"Gene, I don't want to sound insensitive but, you know he's black too, right?" Kody said. Discussing race always made him feel uncomfortable, hot, sweaty, and afraid that he was going to offend his best friend or some random person walking by who might overhear.

"Kody, please," Gene said as he cleaned his glasses on his shirt. "I've seen white people with tans darker than Mr.

Jennings."

Kody stared at him in silence.

Gene broke out in laughter. "Relax! I'm just messing around. I like seeing how uncomfortable it makes you."

"Only because we're in the cafeteria. When it's just us I know you don't care because we're best buds." Kody poked his food with the plastic fork.

Gene, putting his glasses back on, noticed a small tear in Kody's shirt. "I see that you were in another fracas."

Kody deflected. "Nah, clothes from the thrift store don't last like they used to. This shirt probably had a tear in it already and I just didn't realize it."

Gene leaned in and flipped a small magnifying lens down over his glasses to inspect the shirt further. "Judging by the lack of wear on the fibers, that tear appears to be recent."

"Ok, so what if it is?" Kody should've known he couldn't get one by his genius friend. Gene was in tune with every little detail about everything. "We were playing football in gym today. I scored a touchdown and some of the guys got upset. No big deal."

"I do not claim to be an expert on athletics, but is that not an infraction of the rules?" Gene thought for a moment and then said, "Unnecessary roughness. Why didn't Mr. Maris call a penalty on them?" Gene looked at him sternly, like a concerned father in the body of a twelve-year-old boy.

"Dude, relax, hitting people is part of football. Besides, it was the end of class. No big deal. It didn't even hurt, actually. I was more surprised than anything else."

"And you didn't retaliate?"

"You know I can't do that. I'm in enough trouble as it is for what happened in chemistry," Kody said.

"Yes," Gene recalled. "Considering you were not enrolled in chemistry to begin with, you can understand why the instructor was angry."

"First off, I thought it was my study hall," Kody said. "Room three-oh-eight looks a lot like three-hundred if you look at it quick enough. Point number 'B', yellow and blue make green. It's been like that since colors were invented! How was I supposed to know chemicals and colors have different rules?" Kody raised his hands in defense. "Aren't you the one always telling me I should open my mind to new things? Besides, I offered to replace the table-top, I can just make one in woodshop."

"Kody, you were expelled from woodshop after the incident with the varnish. Also, you're getting off-topic. If you recall, we were talking about gym class? Torn clothes ring a bell?"

"Don't be silly, torn clothes can't ring a bell."

"Kody."

Kody shrugged. "Right. Well, what good would it do to fight back? As we've already discussed, after my adventures in woodshop and chemistry, I can't risk getting in more trouble. People always say to try diplomacy, so I tried talking to them, but that just made matters worse!"

"I have experienced your attempts at diplomacy."

"And?"

"And I am confident the Bannerville debate team won't be extending you an invitation."

"Whatever!" Kody exclaimed, laughing. "Anyway," he said, lowering his voice, "when they hit me, it didn't even hurt."

"It didn't...hurt?" Gene raised an eyebrow. He knew his friend was a tough kid, but he was also a bit prideful. This was probably just an exaggeration but he wanted to make sure.

"Seriously. They kicked and punched me but it was just a 'thumping' feeling. No pain. Sure, my clothes got torn and stuff, but I get them at the thrift store, so that's no big deal. The point is, I'm okay for some reason." Kody thought for a moment. "It's kind of weird, actually."

"Hey, hero, is anyone sitting here?" Callie Cruz smiled as she pulled up a chair and sat down next to Kody. She was the second of Kody's two best friends in school. Out of the three of them, she was probably the most normal. Although she was the only one brave enough to try the school's meatloaf, which just the sight of was enough to make most people's stomach turn.

"Lay off the hero stuff, will you?" he said. "I'm not anything like the ones on the news, with cool powers and fancy costumes." The heroes were the only reason Kody watched the news. Getting a chance to see a clip of The Meteor in action was something special. He hoped someday Port Haven would be in enough danger to get his attention.

And Quantum. Kody would love to meet her in person someday.

As an avid reader of comic books, he dreamed of being a superhero, but actually being called one by a friend sounded weird. It's not like he rescued Callie from the clutches of aliens, or stopped a demigod from conquering Earth.

Callie snapped her fingers, "Hey, come back to us, will you?"

"Probably daydreaming about Quantum again." Gene said, rolling his eyes.

"Sorry," Kody said as he realized he left them for a moment. "I got lost again."

"It's okay," she said. "But ever since you got those creeps to stop harassing me at the library last summer, you *are* my hero."

"I don't know if being their punching bag counts," Kody laughed.

"Well, it was still a victory," she said. "More or less."

"More like a moral victory," Kody replied. His caretaker, mentor, and Aikido instructor, Shihan Toshihiro, told him that, in combat, moral victories were *'bad for the body; good for the soul.'*

Kody often dreamed of doing things he saw in the movies, or on the news whenever The Meteor, Quantum, or even Solar and Polar would do something heroic. In his dreams he never lost a fight, and always stopped the bad guy. He would stand victorious in front of a cheering crowd.

The Mayor would give him a medal, and name him protector of Port Haven. Then, when it was discovered that the Mayor was actually--

"Kody!" Callie waved her hands in his face.

"What?"

"You zoned out. Again!"

"Sorry." Normally Kody would be embarrassed to have back-to-back episodes like that, but these were his friends. They understood. "What did you say? Were we still talking about me saving you?"

"Yes. You saved me like a knight in shining armor that day. Maybe I should refer to you as my knight instead of a hero?" Callie waved her plastic fork in the air like a sword.

"Eh, I'll take a cape over a suit of armor any day," he muttered under his breath.

"Callie," Gene scooted his chair away from her. "Please stop swinging that fork before someone loses an eye!" Adjusting his glasses, he added, "That is not a sword and your meatloaf is not a dragon."

"Yeah." Kody pointed at the slice of half-burnt hamburger, covered in ketchup. "You'll be lucky if the fork doesn't break when you stab into it."

"¡Eres carne muerta!" Callie threatened, before jabbing the plastic fork into it. She tried to pull it out, but it wouldn't budge. Awkwardly she looked around and then shouted, "Victory!" Callie held both arms in the air. She nodded her head in approval as Kody cupped his hands over his mouth and mimicked the sound of a cheering crowd.

The two of them broke into laughter.

Gene, on the other hand, slouched down in his seat. He tried to cover his embarrassment by holding a hand to the side of his face. "This is the reason people make fun of us." He looked at the meatloaf on Callie's tray and then at his friends. "Honestly you two need to grow up."

Suddenly, the cafeteria grew quiet.

"Well," Callie said. "That's awkward."

Kody felt several people standing over him, and he

closed his eyes in frustration.

Kody didn't have to look to know that it was Brett, Paulie, and Jared. They apparently weren't satisfied with how things had been left in gym class. Kody picked at his food and tried to ignore them, hoping they would lose interest and go away.

Callie looked up. "Leave us alone. We aren't bothering anyone."

"Callie, please don't," Kody said. The last thing he wanted was for her to get involved.

Gene shouted something about having Kody's back, before diving under the table.

Brett looked at Callie in a way that made her feel vulnerable. "Yeah, Callie, don't. How about you carry my books for the rest of the day instead, and I'll leave your thrift store freak of a boyfriend alone." Reaching out he grabbed Callie by the wrist, pulling her away from the table. Paulie and Jared reached out to help.

"Leave her alone!" Kody shot up from his chair. "You have a problem with me, then take it up with me. But leave my friends out of it." Kody clenched his fists and stared Brett square in the eyes. His heart pounded in his chest.

Brett laughed, "What are you going to do? Come on, loser. Let's see what you got." Brett held his hands out wide, offering an open target for Kody to hit.

"Kody!" Callie yelled as she struggled to free herself from Jared and Paulie's grip. She started shouting at them in Spanish. Insults, most likely, Kody thought.

The cafeteria erupted with shouting. Some kids stood on their chairs to see, as others crowded around to block any teachers from being able to break it up. Kody jerked his shoulder back like he was going to take a swing.

He smiled when Brett flinched.

"I don't want to fight you," Kody said. "And I don't think you want to fight me, either. You're just trying to look cool in front of your friends. I get it. You guys are tougher, cooler and more popular than us. Point taken. So please, just let her go."

Instead, Brett just laughed, "Check it out guys, he can't do it. He's too chicken. Maybe she'll fight me instead." Jared and Paulie start laughing.

"Looks like she wants to," Paulie said as he struggled to hold her still.

"Come on guys," Brett said as he turned his back to Kody. "We need to get moving if this illegal immigrant is going to carry our books." His friends laughed as they started hanging their backpacks around her neck.

Callie's face turned red and she stomped her heel on Jared's foot. "*¡Vaya al infierno!*" she shouted.

"Ahh! Are you dumb? I'll destroy you!" Jared shoved Callie to the ground.

Without thinking, Kody shoved Jared aside, but that gave Brett the moment he needed to punch Kody square in the jaw.

Kody fell backward on the old table, causing it to buckle slightly. He touched his jaw, confused. It didn't hurt!

Brett, however, was clenching his hand. Wincing, his expression was ripe with anger but there was also a bit of confusion in his eyes. He cried out in pain. "I--I think he broke my hand!"

Kody raised an eyebrow. He was the one that got hit. Shouldn't he be the one in pain? "Are, you okay?" he asked, pulling himself off the table.

Jared dove at him, but the lumbering linebacker was too slow.

Stepping aside, Kody placed a hand on Jared's back and shoved him forward. It was a basic defensive maneuver; using his attacker's own momentum against him. Jared's face landed on Callie's ketchup covered meatloaf.

There was a moment of silence as the table creaked under his weight. Then, almost as if it were in slow motion, it snapped in half, collapsing to the floor with a loud crash.

Gene yelped from underneath, safely tucked under the space created by the legs of the table.

Jared lay there, groaning in pain.

Paulie jumped on Kody's back and put him in a headlock, cutting off his air. Kody felt his neck being squeezed tightly. The screaming and chanting all around them became muffled. Blinking his eyes, he tried to clear his thoughts. Gasping for air, his vision started to fade. Panicking, Kody drove his elbow directly into Paulie's stomach, causing him to let go.

Kody paused a moment to catch his breath. Paulie charged him, only to be met by a sidekick to the chest. His eyes went wide as he fell to the floor. Coughing and wheezing, he rolled onto his stomach and curled into a ball.

Kody stood ready to defend himself, looking around in panic, expecting someone else to jump in. He saw a look of fear in Callie's eyes. The sound of students cheering was being drowned out by the sound of his own heart pounding in his chest.

He had downed all three of the bullies.

He began to think maybe he should have done this a long time ago. It was liberating. Those jerks had it coming, and he was the hero who stopped them all. Listening to the crowd of students cheering, he smiled. Was this the moment he'd been waiting for?

Then he saw Paulie being handed an inhaler out of his backpack by another student. Suddenly his excitement turned to guilt.

Paulie has asthma?

Callie pushed her way through the crowd of students, running from the cafeteria.

"Callie, wait!" he called after her.

"Mr. Haywood!" A deep voice boomed and silenced the crowd permanently.

Winters is coming.

Dean Winters seemed to enjoy the attention that came with the sound of his own voice. He walked with a swagger, in his dark suit, unbuttoned dress shirt, and slick, pepper-colored, hair. Everyone knew to stay out of his way.

Kody tried to explain himself, but couldn't get any words out. It was like he suddenly forgot how to talk.

"You have seriously injured three of your fellow students, violated school policy, and damaged school property!" The Dean pointed to the table that broke Jared's fall. He went on to say more, but Kody became entangled in a web of his own thoughts.

The Dean always seemed to show up when Kody got in trouble. If he had an arch-nemesis in the school, it would be the Dean. After the chemistry incident, Winters told him he was in 'hot water.' When Kody asked if he saw the irony in that, things only got worse.

At this moment, Kody thought he was doing the right thing. They were being picked on and harassed, and he just wanted Brett and his goons go away. Why should those goons be allowed to push his friends around but he gets in trouble for pushing back?

He wished good choices were easier to make.

Gene appeared from under the table and handed Kody his backpack, "Here. There is a high probability that you will need this."

"I thought you said you had my back?"

"Pack. I had your backpack."

"That's not what you said."

"Well, that's what I meant to say."

Kody and Gene met by the flagpole behind the school, as the friends did every day after the final bell, and waited in uncomfortable silence. Their peers walked by, glancing over at Kody while whispering to each other.

As they watched everyone else climb aboard their buses or get picked up by their parents, Callie was nowhere to be found.

Kody's heart sank. He had two best friends in this whole world, and Callie was always the one he leaned on for comfort and support. Gene's analytical mind was great for equations and logical thinking, but on a personal level there was a lot he didn't understand about human emotions.

There was silence between the two boys as they made

their way home. Kody slowly weaved back and forth down the empty street on his skateboard. Parallel to him, and covered head-to-toe in safety gear, Gene rode his bike with caution on the sidewalk.

After waiting for as long as he possibly could, Gene asked, "Detention?"

"Yup. For the whole week! Wait, how did you know?"

"If you read the student handbook you would know that on page thirty-two, paragraph three, under 'code of conduct', it has all the information on-"

"Gene, nobody reads the student handbook, come on."

"I did. Also, when I hacked into the school's database, I noticed your name on the detention list."

"And there it is!" Kody exclaimed, knowing there was more to it than just reading the handbook. "Someday you're going to get in trouble for doing that. How am I going to explain this to Shihan?" He gave an angry kick off the pavement to keep his forward momentum, "I didn't mean to hurt them. You know me, Gene. I wouldn't do that on purpose!"

"Yes, I know. All that being said, you seemed pretty resilient. It was as though nothing they did had a negative effect on you." Gene focused on pedaling with great intent. His knuckles were white as he gripped the handlebar, weaving around the sidewalk and trying to avoid every crack and divot.

Kody stopped in the middle of the road in front of Callie's house, and let out a sigh.

Gene stopped pedaling and adjusted his glasses. "Was it something I said?"

"Yes. It *was* something you said. How did you know I wasn't hurt?"

"You can learn a lot from observing the world around you. Or, in this case, the school cafeteria from underneath a broken table," Gene said with a smile. He took the opportunity to adjust his elbow pads and wrist guards.

"Well, you're right. It's like they were slapping me with

a roll of paper towels. I felt the impact but that's it."

And just like that, it wasn't just his secret anymore. He could've just laughed it off and called Gene crazy. Kody knew at some point, though, the genius would figure it out. He trusted his friend not to turn him into a lab rat, so if anyone else was going to know about it; it had to be Gene.

"Do you think she's home already?" Kody asked.

Gene looked over his shoulder. "I doubt it. There's a high probability that even though her father may have picked her up, they aren't home yet. Most likely, they had errands to run. I've observed that when they're home, the car is in the garage with the door open."

"I wouldn't even know what to say to her. I doubt she'll ever talk to me again."

"I hear sirens." Gene looked around nervously. "You should probably get out of the road."

Kody stepped off his skateboard and kicked it up into his hands, carrying it over to the sidewalk. The two of them continued on as the sirens grew louder.

Kody and Gene stopped in their tracks when a small dog darted out in front of them and into the street. Its leash was dragging on the ground behind it. 'Chompers' was an annoying chihuahua owned by the people who lived in the house next to Callie. They watched as she made it across the street, just as a car came screeching around the corner.

The engine roared as the car recovered from its backend fishtailing from the hard turn. Smoke billowed out from the rear wheel wells. It almost appeared as if there was a smoke bomb set off in the trunk.

"Chompers, come back!' A little girl darted out past the two boys and into the road with her arms held out. Chompers sat on the other side of the road, scratching himself; the dog's ears perked up at the sound of its name.

"Look out!" Gene hollered as he saw the car barreling down the road.

Kody sprang into action. He ran after her with his skateboard. He scooped her up and set her onto the board, then gave it a push towards the sidewalk, sending her safely out of the car's path.

He felt the impact of the car against his hip and rib cage.

Everything moved in slow motion as he rolled over the hood, slammed into the windshield, and bounced up and over the roof of the car. Instinctively, he reached out for something to hold onto, and found himself gripping the cutout of the moonroof.

Looking back, he saw the girl crying on the side of the road. She was safe.

"Hey boss, we gotta tagalong!" someone shouted from inside the car. Kody could barely make out the words over the roar of the engine.

"How the-? Finish him off!"

Something began cracking against Kody's fingers, but he held on tightly.

"He ain't lettin' go!"

"Shoot the little prick!"

Kody struggled to maintain his grip as the car swerved around a corner. When a handgun appeared in front of his face, he grabbed onto it and pointed it away from himself just before the gun fired.

As he wrestled with the handgun, Kody remained patient. They turned down a dead-end street. The cops would have them trapped and he would be a hero! Even though he had no clue who these guys were and why they were being chased.

Murder? Armed Robbery? The list of possible crimes was endless.

As Kody's mind began to wander, the car screeched to a stop. He flew off the hood and rolled onto the ground; hitting the concrete barricade that blocked the end of the road. Angry with himself, he dusted off his clothes and stood up.

Kody looked at the two men in the car. They stared back at him from behind their cracked windshield. The driver was furious as he revved the engine.

It was a stand-off.

"Sorry fellas," Kody said in the most heroic voice he could manage, "It's the end of the ro-"

The engine roared, and the back end of the car spewed forth exhaust and burned rubber. Summoning all of the car's horsepower, the driver worked the gas pedal and stick shift to spin the vehicle completely around.

Kody stood in a gray cloud of dust and fumes, coughing and gasping for air. "Come on!" He said as he tried to catch his breath, "That was...going to be an epic...one-liner!"

As the smoke cleared, he rubbed the sting out of his eyes and began walking back to where he left Gene. The boy genius was cautiously pedaling his bicycle while holding the skateboard across his legs.

"That was amazing!" Gene said as he got off his bike.

"Amazing? Did you miss the part where I got hit by a car?"

After deploying the kickstand, Gene handed Kody the skateboard, "Did it hurt?"

"No," Kody admitted. "It hurts more that I didn't get to say my one-liner. It was going to be smart and funny!"

Gene rolled his eyes. "Yeah, okay."

"Did they get away?" Kody asked while setting his skateboard on the ground, "What direction did they go in?"

Gene shrugged his shoulders, "They blew right by me. I was more focused on your condition than tracking a car you can't catch. Let the police handle it. This—" Gene said as he waved his hands at his friend, "—is unprecedented! Your durability is a scientific anomaly!" Gene walked around Kody and inspected him for any signs of injury.

All he saw were tattered clothes.

"How exciting!" Gene squealed.

"I wouldn't say it's exciting." Kody scratched his head to rid his hair of dirt and stone. "I mean, the guy aimed a gun at my face, dude. My. *Face*!"

"Did he shoot your face?" Gene grabbed Kody's cheeks and pulled the taller boy down for a closer inspection.

Kody raised an eyebrow. "Ish that conshern, or enthushiashm?"

"Can it be both?"

Kody brushed his friend's hands aside. "No. He didn't shoot me in the face." It was one thing to get in a fight at school and come out unscathed, but this was different. He replayed what happened in his head. It all happened so fast! But here he stood, unharmed in front of his friend who saw it all unfold. "Gene?"

"Yes?" Gene shifted his glasses and continued to inspect his friend by looking closely at Kody's forearm.

"What's happening to me?"

"From my initial observations, I would say that you are indestructible. But, without more testing, one could argue that it's a series of fortunate events leading to a wild set of coincidences." Gene stood up and rested his chin on his thumb. "I'd like to run a few experiments."

"Experiments? I'm not a lab rat, dude. You just saw what happened!" Kody pointed to the barrier he was thrown against when the car skidded to a halt. "I don't know what else you need to see. From what I can tell I *am* indestructible. I should be dead right now."

"It's true. But we need to know why. We need to understand if it's something you accidentally did in chemistry, or if it's just a part of who you are. Your birthday is coming up. I wonder if it's something that's in your DNA and it finally manifested." Gene got back on his bike and looked at Kody. "C'mon, let's go."

"Go where?"

"To my house!" Gene shouted as he pedaled off.

Kody had never seen the boy pedal so quickly. The boy who was always very careful not to get hurt riding on his bike was now racing furiously against time.

"Hey, wait up!" Kody called after his friend, who had a big head start. "There aren't going to be any needles are there? Because I don't like needles!" He kicked off the pavement to chase after Gene on his skateboard.

"Even if there were, it seems they would be ineffective!" Gene hollered back.

"I see your point!" Kody replied. He thought about that for a moment. "Ha! Get it? Needle! Point!"

Even though he hadn't yet caught up to his younger friend, he knew Gene's eyes were rolling. As he rolled by Callie's house again, he wondered once more if she was home and if she was still mad at him. She hadn't answered any of his texts, which made him nervous. What was different about him saving her this time, as opposed to what happened before?

Over the summer, he stood up for her and became a punching bag. This time, he did the same thing and took down the bullies. It didn't seem fair that losing was a win and winning was a loss.

Being a hero, he thought, was far more complicated than it should be.

Kody raised an eyebrow and pointed to the doors. "Are we doing this down there?"

Gene only nodded and motioned for Kody to follow him down the steps and into the darkness that filled his parent's storm cellar.

The steps were narrow and there was a musty smell in the air that almost made Kody gag. "Why can't we just go to your room? You know, inside the house?" He pleaded, "I mean, I was kind of hoping we'd do this really quick, and then maybe play some video games. Oh, and have your mom make us some sandwiches or something."

"You presume far too much; one thing being that my mom is home and another that she would make us sandwiches." Gene tugged at a string which clicked on a light.

Kody looked around and saw that he was surrounded by shelves full of wine bottles.

Putting his hand on one of the dust-covered bottles, Gene paused. "You are not the only one with a secret."

"You're an alcoholic?" He touched one of the dusty bottles, then rubbed his fingers against his hoodie. "We can get you help, I promise. It's got to be hard being twelve and in high school."

"Do not be so naïve. I don't have the slightest desire to drink alcohol." He pulled down on the bottle, and the wall began to vibrate. The bricks separated, and opened up like a door, revealing a well-lit room inside. Gene motioned for Kody to follow him.

"What the-?" For the first time he could remember, Kody was speechless.

After they were inside, Gene gently pulled the wall shut behind them.

It was a small, well-organized room accommodating various equipment. There was an old folding table running along the length of the back wall, a chair positioned in the middle. On the table were three display monitors; on the floor, the biggest hard drives Kody had ever seen, each was resting on a wooden pallet. Different colored lights flashed intermittently.

There was a bookshelf and a three-drawer filing cabinet on the opposite wall. In between those sat a smaller table with a weird looking microscope and some other gadgets that weren't familiar to Kody. The microscope had wires leading out of it and up the wall, across the ceiling and back down to the computers.

"I have been dissatisfied with the quality of the equipment my parents provide me." Gene sat down in the chair and turned on each computer monitor from left to right. "So, I have been mining crypto-currency, and occasionally selling some of it off to cash in to make real-world investments that deliver healthy returns to my financial portfolio."

"Wow," Kody said, scratching his head. "So, you bought a whole bunch of new stuff?"

"Please. I could not just buy this stuff. Not for how I plan to use them, that would be far too expensive. Not to mention the highly specific combination of pre-installed components would have the NSA knocking on my door with a multitude of inquiries."

"Ah. I get it," Kody replied, even though he didn't really get it.

Seeing the confusion on his friend's face, Gene added, "I purchased the parts that I required from different technological resources and built everything in this room. I prefer customization over the walled garden of your average run-of-the-mill computer. I have no desire to work with generic machines filled with bloatware."

Kody thought for a moment. "My dude, I have no clue what you just said. But it sounds pretty awesome." Kody stood behind Gene's chair and looked at the monitors. "So, which one plays the video games?"

"None of them plays 'the video games,' Kody."

"How many people know about this place?"

"Just the two of us." Gene replied sternly, "I prefer to be surreptitious when it comes to these things." Without warning, Gene pulled a pair of tweezers from his pocket and yanked a strand of hair from his friend's head.

Kody rubbed at his scalp. He wasn't expecting to be plucked like a chicken.

Gene placed the hair on a glass slide and slid it under his microscope. Sitting down in the chair, he cranked a lever to raise himself up.

"On the surface, your hair looks fine," he said.

"Thanks, I use conditioner." Kody ran a hand through the shaggy black mess.

Gene lowered his chair. "My statement was not meant to compliment your grooming, but to indicate that I will not find anything out of the ordinary on the surface." Gene moved his chair in front of the monitor to his left and began typing something on his keyboard. "I will need to create a cross-section of the follicle and examine the properties that exist inside it."

"My hair has an inside?"

Gene clicked his mouse and the screen changed. Then he started furiously typing away on his keyboard.

Kody had no clue what was happening, but images began flashing on all three monitors. Things were moving around, changing colors, and objects began appearing, rotating, and flipping.

"Are you playing a video game? Because you said there were no video games." He pulled up a chair and sat down. "I'm going next."

Gene shook his head. Sliding his chair to a different monitor he began typing up a long string of formulas. Clicking, dragging, zooming, typing. He was moving faster and faster as he continued to work. Watching as Gene moved from station to station in his little makeshift lab, he found it amazing what this kid could do.

"So, genius, is this what you do all day?" Gene was smarter than anyone else Kody knew. How could anyone know so much stuff? Kody thought going to school was just a big interruption to his day, whereas Gene looked at school as a way to enhance his day.

Comic books and video games were the only things that Kody cared about. And skateboarding. And helping people. That made him feel important. Callie once told him he should go into public service. He could be a social worker, she said, because he was always trying to help people. She said it was an attractive quality.

Kody figured if being attractive was a requirement to be a social worker, Callie would be more qualified than him.

"Kody?" Gene interrupted his thoughts. "There is definitely something happening on a genetic level here. But it's unnatural. A forced mutation of some kind has occurred within your DNA."

"Meaning?"

"You weren't born this way."

"Meaning?"

Gene took his glasses off and began cleaning them with a small cloth. "Someone did this to you."

Kody looked at the back of his hands. He wasn't sure what he was expecting to see, but he felt the sudden urge to check. "Somebody...*did* this to me?"

"Is that concern, or enthusiasm?" Gene asked.

"Can it be both?" Kody asked. "I mean, I know my older brother Dan was a bit of a jokester, but I don't think slipping toxic sludge in my oatmeal was on the table." He pulled out his phone. "I'm going to ask him."

"No!" Gene snatched the phone away. "This is not something we should just start telling everyone about. This isn't some comic book where everyone keeps a secret, just because. There are real implications here."

"Okay, then distract me with an explanation. If I wasn't born this way, how did I get a mutation?" Kody took his phone back and slipped it into his pocket.

Gene took a deep breath, knowing he would probably lose Kody halfway through what he was about to say. But he wasn't going to let that stop him from trying. "Genetic mutations, by definition, are not as uncommon as you may think. Any gene that undergoes a change, which affects the transmission or expression of a trait, is considered 'mutated'. This could result in someone being extremely tall in a typically short family. The gene that determines their height was mutated when the DNA strand was being built. Or, to better explain it on your level, the child would be born with a tall gene."

Kody scratched at his head. "So, if a peace-loving family had a kid that constantly got into fights, that kid has the mean gene?"

"Okay, I'm impressed you followed along." Gene was pleasantly surprised. It was a small victory. "You have the right idea. Poor analogy, but right idea."

Kody smiled. "And if a family of dirty people gave birth to a neat freak, that child would have the clean gene?"

"What are you doing?"

"Wait! Does that mean environmentalists have the green gene?"

"Ugh, seriously?" Gene looked up in frustration. Maybe Kody wasn't listening after all. "Labeling a gene, based on an individual's ideology, is not the same as understanding a highly complicated piece of the human genome!"

"Sheesh, I think you may have the scream gene," Kody muttered under his breath.

"Excuse me?" The irritation in Gene's voice stabbed at Kody's good judgment.

"Nothing!" Kody dismissed. He instinctively turned to see Callie's expression and was immediately disheartened by her absence. She would've thought it was funny. He checked his phone to see that she still hadn't texted him.

"Now, if you're done being silly," Gene paused to collect his thoughts, "we need to find out who, or what, caused the mutation."

Kody frowned. The thought of someone using him as an experiment made his hair stand on end.

Except for the one that his friend yanked out, of course.

"I'd like to perform a few tests on you to discover the root of this puzzle." The boy genius stood up and pressed his fingers into Kody's chest.

"What kind of tests?"

Gene walked around and began doodling in the air with his finger and then nodded with confidence. "I have your hair sample, which can provide me with a significant amount of information. However, this will take a while to decipher. I will need to perform a plethora of tests, actually. Rome was not built in a day, you know."

"Rome?" Kody asked. "Is that the first part of the test? I don't know how many days it took to build Rome. A month maybe? I'm not very good at history. Or math."

Gene shook his head and responded through clenched teeth. "No, that's not the test, it was just an expression. A figure of speech. Something you would realize if you paid any attention to what I say to you."

"Okay, okay! Chill out, genius." Kody threw his hands up in defense. "I'm starting to think you might have the 'mean' gene. Oh, that's funny because your name-"

"Just don't," Gene interrupted, "I am already starting to reconsider this partnership," he grumbled.

Kody's phone buzzed.

"Oh, perhaps you are being called home?" Gene's voice was as hopeful as it had ever sounded.

Kody looked at his phone. "It's Callie. She wants to talk."

"Then I recommend you go to her." Gene turned back to his monitors as Kody got up to leave. "And take your time. As a matter of fact, I'll call you when I'm done. No need to check in."

When Kody arrived at Callie's, he frowned at seeing her dad's car in the garage. Mr. Cruz had an alcohol problem and spent a lot of time at the bars drinking. So, naturally, he would choose tonight of all nights to stay home after they were done with errands.

Kody tossed his skateboard behind the shrubs as he made his way around to the back of the house. In the backyard, there was a tall maple tree he and Callie would sit in. The window shade to her room was closed, but he could hear Mr. Cruz yelling. He couldn't make out what was being said, but it was loud enough to hear that thick Hispanic accent. There were things being thrown and, thankfully, it didn't sound like Callie was one of them.

The situation put Kody on edge, and he thought for a brief second sitting in the tree was a bad idea. It seemed like he waited a lifetime before the yelling stopped. When it did, he was startled to see the shade and window open so quickly.

"Oh!" Callie jumped back, startled to see her friend. "How long have you been here?"

"Not long," he lied.

He offered her a hand to help her out onto the branch. There was a moment of awkward silence before they both said, "I wanted to-"

"Um, you go first," Callie offered as she looked down, tucking a lock of pecan colored hair behind her ear.

"You sure?"

"Yeah."

"Okay." Kody took a breath. "I wanted to apologize for my behavior at school. I shouldn't have fought those jerks, but I couldn't just sit by and watch you be treated like that. But then I get here, and now I'm more concerned about your situation."

"Don't be," she said. "My dad's just drinking again. I guess he decided not to go to the bar before work, so he's elbow deep in the cooler. It's fine, really. I'm used to it."

Kody couldn't help but notice the sadness in her eyes. "It's not fine," he said out of frustration. "I wish you could get away from him." He wondered what his own father was like. Was he a heavy drinker? Was he violent? Kody didn't like to judge Callie's dad because he had never met his own, but he was pretty confident Mr. Cruz wasn't a candidate for father of the year. His father couldn't possibly be worse than an abusive alcoholic.

"So," Callie was quick to change the subject. "About what happened at school. I'm sorry I ran off, but you really scared me. I had never seen you like that before, and I guess I just needed to process it. I mean, I've seen you deal with bullies, but this was different. This time you got violent. It almost looked like you were enjoying yourself. And that's not the Kody I know." She put her hand on his back, "You don't enjoy hurting people. At least, I hope not."

Kody felt warm from her touch. It was almost enough to make him forget why he was there.

"I don't enjoy it!" he exclaimed. "I just want to be something to someone. I want to," he paused because saying 'be a hero' sounded dumb in his head. Which means it probably sounded even dumber out loud. "I don't know how to explain it."

She smiled. "Listen, you don't have to prove anything to anyone. You are one of the nicest, sweetest people I know. And even though it's hard to avoid trouble, in a school that's full of it, all we can do is be the best version of ourselves. Don't worry about what everyone else thinks. Be you, and good people will surround you."

Kody smiled back, "Deal." He nudged her playfully with his shoulder, "If someone starts messing with me again, I'll just have Gene save me."

Callie laughed. "The only thing he can save you from is bad grades!"

Kody's cell phone buzzed in his pocket. He pulled it out to see that Gene found something. "Speak of the devil," Kody said. "It's getting kind of late. I should probably see what he wants and then head home. Shihan Toshihiro doesn't like it when I get to my loft too late. He says I stomp around like a gorilla and it sounds like the whole dojo is coming down."

"Okay. I'll see you tomorrow at school then?" Callie leaned in and gave Kody a quick hug before climbing back into her bedroom window.

Down below, the back door opened. Callie's father stepped out onto the patio. Kody looked down and saw something in his left hand. It was getting dark, and he couldn't quite make out what it was.

"What're you doin' in my tree?" Mr. Cruz shouted.

"Nothing, sir," Kody said respectfully. "I'm getting down now."

"Yer talkin' to my baby girl aren't you! Hey girl, are you up in dat tree with the boy?" Mr. Cruz took a few drunken steps out further onto the patio and looked up. His eyes widened when he realized Callie's window was open. "You tryin' to hurt my baby girl?" He took another step and stumbled.

Callie poked her head out from her window. "Papi, stop it!"

The two of them began arguing with each other in their native tongue.

Kody used that opportunity to try and sneak away. He began moving down the branch, working his way to a point where he was low enough to drop down. He looked down to make sure his feet were secure on the branches before putting his weight on them. He had done this a hundred times before, but having Callie's father standing there was making him nervous.

"Where do you think you're going, boy? You can't just sneak onto my property like that! What were you gonna do, huh? Try and hurt my baby girl?" Kody took his eyes off his feet and looked over at Mr. Cruz who was waving something at him, as he continued shouting, switching between Spanish and English.

"What? No, I was just talking! I'm getting down now, I swear!" Kody hurried his pace but forgot to check his footing. His left foot caught a dead branch and it snapped, causing him to slip. Kody grabbed at the tree to catch himself, and hung dangling from another branch.

The noise startled Mr. Cruz as he stepped back and stumbled.

BANG!

A gunshot pierced the air, and Kody felt the impact of the bullet in his back. He lost his grip and fell.

"Kody!" He heard Callie scream, and several dogs in the neighborhood started barking before he hit the ground.

Kody lay there for a moment, confused. Callie was screaming and her father was swearing at her. Rolling over, he picked himself up and dusted himself off. He was angry that Callie's father had shot him, but surprisingly enough he wasn't at all hurt. When he realized that Callie was outside on the patio arguing with her father, he wondered if maybe he blacked out for a moment.

"Oh my God, Kody are you okay?" Callie tried to approach him, but her dad grabbed her by the arm.

"Don't you go near that boy!"

"Papi, let go!" Callie struggled to break free, but despite his drunkenness, her father's grip was well trained.

"I'm fine. Don't worry!" Kody said as he began to back

away. "No harm, no foul right? I won't talk about it if you don't." He didn't like how Mr. Cruz was handling Callie, but it wasn't his place to get involved. Based on the stories she'd told him in the past, this was actually pretty tame.

Instead of intervening, Kody ran around to the side of the house, snatched up his skateboard, and ran to the street without stopping. Once he got to the sidewalk, he tossed the board out in front of himself and jumped on it to race home.

He needed to call Gene!

He pulled the cell phone out of his hoodie pocket and speed-dialed his friend.

Gene picked up as though he had been waiting for the call. "Hello Kody. I was just getting ready to call you to share some amazing findings!"

"Gene, listen to me. I just got shot!" Kody exclaimed. He quickly looked around, hoping there wasn't anyone who had heard him. He pushed off the ground to accelerate his skateboard further.

"What?" Gene's voice squeaked on the other end. "Where are you? I thought you went to talk with Callie?"

"I did! I went to Callie's to apologize about this afternoon. Her dad was drinking and he thought I was some crook trying to break in or something. The point is," he paused to swallow hard and take a breath, "he friggin' shot-" Kody stopped himself, remembering what Gene said earlier about other people knowing. He looked around, then lowered his voice to a whisper, "Mr. Cruz shot me."

Kody could hear him tapping away on his keyboard. No doubt the boy genius was making notes and calculations and whatever else it was that smart people did with information.

"That is fantastic!" Gene was so excited he could barely contain himself. "Are you injured? Was there epidermal penetration? Perhaps even just a mild contusion?"

"I have no clue what you just said, but I'm not bleeding and it doesn't hurt. I just had to tell someone and, well...you're the only one that knows about my situation."

He hoped he had made the right decision by talking to Gene.

"You do realize I will not be able to obtain the recommended hours of sleep now!"

"Tell me about it." Kody couldn't tell if Gene was angry or excited. It didn't really matter to him, as long as his friend was able to get some answers.

"We shall reconvene tomorrow, and I will share my findings with you. If anything else happens, make sure you let me know. Every bit of information is vital to learning more about your condition."

"Condition? I'm not sick, Gene, I'm…" A chill went down his spine. It was as though his skin was a suit of armor. "I'm friggin' BULLETPROOF!"

"Yes, it appears that way."

There was some silence between the two of them as Gene continued to work on the other end of the call. Kody didn't have anything left to say. He felt like he wanted to say more, but he wasn't sure there was anything to add.

"I'm bulletproof." The words just slipped out of his mouth.

"Yes," Gene said. "We've established that."

"Gene, aren't you impressed? Like, this is crazy dude."

"I am extremely impressed, but too much time is wasted on things we already know," Gene replied. "It's time to shift our focus to discovering the unknown."

"Right. Okay, so I'll see you at school. Hey, which reminds me, where are we going to sit in lunch now that our table is broken?"

"We'll have to ask someone to let us sit with them. Or, maybe they'll just be afraid of you and slide over!" Gene liked the idea of people being afraid of them for a change.

"I'm not a bully."

"I know that," Gene said. "You know that. But I have a feeling we'll be able to find a new place to sit. Who is going to challenge you and say no?"

"Somebody will. You think boxing, wrestling, or mixed

martial arts champs never get challenged? People are always out to prove they can beat the best." Kody shuddered to think of it. "I probably have a target on my back right now. Especially with other kids on the football team. Their season may be in trouble! That's going to make them angry at me."

"Nobody is going to target you," Gene assured him. "Not at school, anyway. They always increase security in the lunch room when there's been a fight."

"Yeah, I guess you're right there."

"It happens a lot." Gene said with an air of confidence in his voice.

Kody got off the phone with Gene and went around to the back of the building he called home. There was a fire escape that led up to his loft, which was also above Shihan Toshihiro's Aikido school. The light from the sign illuminated him, as the sun had given way to the night sky.

He hadn't realized how late it was and while he may be bulletproof, his ears weren't soundproof. There was no way he wanted to deal with Shihan Toshihiro if he got caught coming in so late. Thankfully, he was still probably teaching his last class of the evening.

He entered his loft and closed the door softly behind him, taking a deep breath and holding it to listen. After a few seconds, he finally let out a heavy sigh.

He couldn't believe the day he just had. There was so much to think about, and he couldn't talk about it with anyone but Gene. And he had already done that.

Part of him wanted to jump out of his window, just to see what would happen. The other part wanted to curl up into a ball and disappear. Feeling cold and alone, he pulled an old comforter around his shoulders and opened up his flip phone. Just seeing the names of his contacts made him feel a bit warmer.

There was a knock on his door.

"Kody!" It was Shihan Toshihiro. "Kody, you in there?"

He jumped off the sofa, startled. Opening the door, he

looked down at the short, bald, Asian man, who was stroking his long white beard. Shihan was a strange little Japanese man who spoke broken English. Sometimes it was hard to understand him and, on occasion, Kody would poke fun at his attempts to speak full sentences. He always seemed to leave out words, as if they were unnecessary and he was in a hurry.

"I was just finishing up some, um, homework."

"You are bad liar." The old man turned and walked away.

"What? No." Kody followed him out into the hallway. "I had some math problems to do. You know how bad I am at math. Got to keep those grades up, right?"

"You no work on homework. You out with friends, getting into trouble."

"Let me guess, you can 'smell' trouble and I stink of it?" He followed Shihan Toshihiro downstairs.

"Hai." The old man confirmed and chuckled under his breath. "Come. You clean dojo now. It also stink."

"Shihan?" Kody said as he removed his shoes to step out onto the mats.

"Yes?"

"Forget it." He picked up the push broom and began sweeping the foyer by the entrance.

"You have bad day at school but don't want to talk about it."

"Yeah, kind of."

"You get into fight with bullies. Very bad. Don't want to disappoint Shihan Toshihiro." The old man took a seat behind the desk and he put on his glasses, only to peer over them as he inspected the bookkeeping for the day.

Kody stopped sweeping. "These kids were harassing me and my friends, and they grabbed Callie and shoved her to the ground. I couldn't let them treat her like that."

"What did you gain by fighting? Did you cultivate respect...or nurture more hatred?"

"Well, to be honest, they probably hate me more. But,

on the other hand, they won't bother us anymore either, that's for sure. So, that counts as a win, right?" Kody began sweeping again, this time with hard, fast strokes.

"Ah, moral victory."

"Yeah, yeah. I know," Kody said. "I'm fine, though. They're the ones who got hurt."

"Hai. But now you make enemy. Will do anything to teach you lesson." Shihan Toshihiro was stroking his beard as he closed the books. "You did not solve problem, only create bigger one. Must learn to understand your enemy. Turn battlefield into common ground."

"I don't want to understand him."

"I bet he say same thing."

"So why do I have to be the nice guy?" Kody set the broom aside and began rolling up the mats. "He's the jerk who started all of this."

"Hate is a weapon. Is important to disarm your opponent." Shihan Toshihiro began heading to the stairs.

"Oh, I get it. Make him think I'm a nice guy, and then when he least expects it…" Kody punched a fist into his hand. "POW!"

"Greatest weapon not your fist or feet," Shihan replied. "Greatest weapon is heart, is brain."

"Yeah, well, it's easier to just punch him in the mouth. Some people can't be reasoned with, you know."

"Is true, but Kody Haywood won't know unless he try. Make sure you turn off lights."

"Wait, where are you going?"

"Shihan Toshihiro try to sleep."

Kody finished closing up the dojo, then headed back upstairs to his loft. He laid his head on a small pillow and stared at the wall until he fell asleep. The last thing in the world he wanted to do was be Brett's friend.

He was more jerk than jock.

Brett couldn't hurt him physically, but Kody realized he may have put his friends in more danger if Brett decided to go after them instead. He couldn't take the chance Gene or

Callie might get hurt.

He had to try and end this nonsense with Brett and his goons. Maybe for starters, he thought, he should stop referring to them as goons.

The next day at school, Kody was directed by his homeroom teacher to report directly to Dean Winters' office. When he got there, the Dean's door was shut and he heard people talking inside. He tried to see who was in there by peeking between two posters that covered the glass window, but it was no good. He thought about peeling one of the posters back, but decided against it. Winters would probably accuse him of destroying even more property if the poster from the school spirit squad had even the tiniest tear in it.

The door to the office opened. Kody quickly turned around and slouched against the wall, attempting to appear as though he had been waiting for a long time. Several teachers walked out of the room, all of whom had Kody as a student at one time or another. As each one walked by him, they gave him a look and shook their head as if to say, *We're so disappointed in you.*

Dean Winters came out of the office and stood in the doorway. He faced Kody, and they locked eyes for a moment. Finally, Winters extended a hand to invite Kody into his office. He did not step aside, forcing Kody to squeeze through uncomfortably.

Once in the office, Kody took a seat in front of the tall man's desk. He noticed black and white pictures scattered about the office, pictures of Dean Winters looking much younger than he was now and dressed in military clothing. Some pictures had the Dean smiling with his buddies. Other pictures were of him holding his rifle with a cigarette dangling from his mouth. There were a few certificates of achievement, several awards, and even a small picture that was taken more recently where he was standing proudly on top of a mountain.

There were no pictures of the Dean's family.

Dean Winters closed his door and made his way to his desk and sat down. Sliding the top drawer of his desk open, he pulled out a small pack of breath mints and popped one in his mouth. Without offering any to Kody, he put the mints back in the drawer and closed it. He leaned forward, folded his hands on the desk, and clicked the breath mint against his teeth.

They sat across from each other as if they were locked in a standoff. The room was silent except for the sound of the clock on the wall behind Winters, and the breath mint.

Tick-Tock, Tick-Tock.

Clickety-clickety-clickety.

Kody shifted uneasily in his seat, wishing the dean would just say something. He didn't even care what. Maybe the dean was waiting for an apology? Kody decided that would be a good place to start. He opened his mouth to speak but Dean Winters cut him off.

"You don't have parents do you mister Haywood? Only a legal guardian. A Mister...Toshi-Toshihiro? Am I saying that correctly?"

Kody ran a hand through his hair. "Yeah, that's him. Shihan Toshihiro. He runs an Aikido sch-"

Dean Winters interrupted. "I wonder what he would say if he knew you injured several of your fellow students."

"Oh, he figured it out. I figured you would've called him anyway. He said I should have talked with Brett and tried to understand why he's always bullying me."

"Bullying?" Dean Winters replied. "I don't think you understand the word, Mr. Haywood. We don't allow bullying in this school, and Brett is an outstanding student, both academically and within the community. Which is why yesterday's incident has put me in a terrible position." Dean Winters leaned back and interlocked his fingers behind his head, still clicking the breath mint between his teeth.

Again, Kody tried to speak and, again, he was cut off.

"I have the parents of three students, students who are all productive, mind you, wanting you removed from this school. Do you know why?"

"Because-,"

"Because you hurt their boys and jeopardized their chances to earn academic scholarships!" Dean Winter interjected. "I don't pretend to think you understand what it's like to have your future threatened because some punk kid with no future decides he can't take a few insults. If they can't finish out the football season, they'll run the risk of missing out on playing when college scouts are in town."

"Well, maybe he-"

"Your grades display a tremendous lack of effort," the dean continued. "You aren't involved in any after-school activities. Would you like to tell me why you come to school every day? Do you come here only to disrupt this academic ecosystem?"

"What?" Kody stammered. "I come here to learn, I guess. I mean, that's what you're supposed to do right? Kids are supposed to go to school and learn things."

Dean Winters nodded his head. "Yes, that's what you're supposed to do. So, answer this question for me, Mr. Haywood." He paused and leaned forward. "Why aren't you learning anything?"

"I am," Kody said defensively. He wasn't sure what game the dean was playing but he was starting to feel uncomfortable. "Sure, I've struggled, but I've never failed any of my classes. Don't I get any credit for that?"

Dean Winters considered that for a moment and then agreed. "Yes, I suppose you do. However, you haven't learned any real lessons. Such as how being disruptive makes it difficult for other students—other students who want to do more than just *learn*," he said, making air quotes with his fingers. "A lot of your peers understand that school is so much more than grades. Your older brother, Dan, understood that as well. If not for him, we wouldn't have college scouts visiting our school. He was a talented athlete and put us on the map…"

Kody sat in silence. He had stopped listening after something was said about his brother. He wished he could leave school and not come back, maybe just drop out and get a job somewhere. Nobody would miss him, except maybe Callie. And Gene. Shihan Toshihiro would need help with the dojo. Okay, he thought, maybe he would be missed. He looked up and noticed Dean Winters was still talking.

"…this isn't some high school musical, where you can sing and tap dance your way without a care in the world. Performing a melodramatic solo in the stairwell about how tough life is won't get you through *real* life. You need to think about your future and how your actions affect other people around you…"

A school musical? What did the drama club have anything to do with his situation, he wondered? He hated attending school plays, but since he hated sitting in class listening to teachers drag on about the days lesson, he supposed they weren't that bad. Maybe he should look into trying out for a role. A musical might be easier to sit through if he was actually in it.

"...when you graduate, you are on your own in this world. Whether you choose a college or a career, your success is dependent on what you've learned in this building. And I can't have you holding other students back because you are in need of attention."

Attention? Kody didn't do things for attention, that he was aware of. He couldn't explain why Brett and his goons were focused on him. They just were.

"Mr. Haywood!" Dean Winters shouted. "Have you heard a single word I've said?"

"I faded in and out," Kody replied with honesty. He didn't mean to, but he had no control over it. There were so many words being spoken that his mind wandered off.

"Your smart mouth is going to get you in a lot of trouble young man."

"I don't have a smart mouth...it's just honest!" Kody protested.

The dean slammed a hand down on his desk. His voice boomed. "Those kids are excellent students with good grades and are involved in after-school programs that benefit the community. Brett is an outstanding student-athlete. Why would he be picking a fight with you when it would risk forfeiting a chance at a scholarship?"

"I don't know, maybe you should ask him that? I'm telling you, they started it," Kody said in his defense. He wanted to challenge the dean to talk with Callie, but dragging her into it was the last thing on his mind. "I'm sorry you're blinded by their grades and extra stuff they do, but they pick on me all the time. I can't continue to just sit around and let that happen. I don't deserve to be treated like a lesser person! Nobody does!"

"Then you need to report what's happening so that I can speak with them," the dean countered. "Hurting your classmates is no way to handle it. This isn't the wild west, and you're no gunslinging vigilante. If it was, and you were,

I'd be the sheriff and nothing would protect you from me keeping the peace. You aren't bulletproof. And I won't tolerate you going after people like it's your job." Dean Winters opened Kody's student conduct file.

"Wait a minute!" Kody pleaded. "I know it was wrong to hit those guys, but it was in self-defense! I didn't go after them! Aren't you going to talk with them about what they did?"

"My conversations with other students are confidential. You need to focus on this one. This is about you right now. Not them." He tapped a finger on his desk in thought. "I believe in redemption, Mr. Haywood. And, against my better judgement, I want to harness your energy and focus it towards something positive." Winters opened a drawer in his desk, pulled out a flyer, and handed it to Kody.

He took it and looked it over, but to him it was just a bunch of jumbled words. He was too stressed to actually read what it said.

"I'm entering you into the Emerging Leaders of Port Haven program after school."

"You want me to be an ELPH?" Kody sunk in his seat. He didn't want to stay after school. He had important things to do.

"Unless of course, you'd prefer that whole week of detention?" Winters slammed the drawer shut. "I'm offering you an opportunity at probation. Lunch detention today and, beginning next week, Emerging Leaders."

Shihan Toshihiro would not be pleased about him having detention for a week. At least this way he could spin it like he's volunteering to help the community. "Okay, okay." Kody conceded. "I'll do the leaders thing if it means I don't have to stay after school in a room with you all week."

"Good," Dean Winters said with a smooth satisfactory tone in his voice. "I believe you have good intentions, Mr. Haywood. You just need some guidance and a way to focus that energy of yours." He sat back and folded his arms across his chest with a smile on his face. "I'll see you at lunch."

Callie was heading to her locker when she heard Kody call out her name. She had been trying to avoid him while she sorted through her thoughts about his visit. She was certain her father accidentally shot him out of the tree. But Kody was unharmed so, clearly, the bullet didn't hit him.

But she saw what she saw.

"Hey Callie," he said as he raced to be by her side.

"Hey, how did your meeting with Dean Winters go?" she asked as she opened her locker and began swapping out books.

"Okay, I guess. Looks like I'm having lunch with him today, and then next week I'm an ELPH." Kody rolled his eyes.

"Um, you do know I'm in that program, right?" Callie said. "It's important to help the community. Especially those less fortunate than us. You like helping people, I'm actually surprised you didn't sign up at the beginning of the school year."

"You know I can't," Kody said. "I need to be home to help Shihan with the Aikido school. He's not getting any younger. Sometimes he can't even find his glasses. He'd be lost without me."

"Don't you usually help after the school is closed?" she asked. "You're like the janitor, Kody. He'll be fine."

"Yeah, but then I won't have time for fun stuff after my homework."

"Kody, you can't always live inside a comic book," Callie said. "Not that there's anything wrong with that but sometimes other things become more important. In your case, Emerging Leaders makes it so you don't have to spend time after school in Dean Winters' office." She shut her locker and smiled. "Plus, you'll be with me!"

They started walking together down the hall towards their next class, "So," Kody asked, hoping to change the subject. "How's it going with you?"

"Oh, everything is fine on my end. I've just been busy making sure all the articles are finalized for the *Bannerville Bugle* next week." Callie never liked talking about her home life, and she could tell Kody was trying to bait her into doing it. It was embarrassing, and being lead editor of the school paper allowed her plenty of other things to talk about. Especially when she needed to change a subject.

Any time she wanted to be left alone, she just hid out in the 'bullpen,' the small room set aside for the school paper. Nobody ever went in there unless they needed to print something.

"I wasn't talking about the paper."

"I am, though," Callie said.

"Right." Kody scratched at his shaggy black hair

nervously. "Don't you write all of the articles?"

"I write most of them," she admitted. "But I have a few extra submissions this week, and I need to make sure they're edited. I may save them for Monday, though, because I've got to focus on finishing an essay for English."

Callie couldn't help but think everyone walking by them in the hallway was staring. She was nervous about being seen with Kody after his altercation. Even though it could be assumed she's just getting the story, there were still dirty looks. Everyone knew they were friends.

A couple of cheerleaders walked by and, after a long stare-down with Callie, immediately set to whispering between themselves. She ignored it because there was something else that was troubling her.

She saw her friend get shot. She was sure of it. She wanted to say something to him about it, but wasn't sure how to bring it up.

"So, you're just focused on getting the paper out?" Kody reaffirmed. "Okay, because I was thinking you were trying to avoid me." And then, as if he was reading her mind, "You know, after your dad shot me and all."

Spoken without a care in the world.

"Are you kidding me right now?" She stopped in her tracks. It shouldn't have surprised her. Kody was as unpredictable as the weather in Port Haven.

"Relax," Kody said in his defense. "He didn't shoot me. I'm just messing with you."

She mustered up the best smile she could, given the circumstances. "Of course. I knew that."

Perhaps she was wrong, but her instincts knew better.

"So... have you been trying to avoid me or what? I was looking for you this morning, and you weren't in the cafeteria for breakfast."

"No," she said. "Maybe. I don't know." Callie was struggling. Not only was she hoping not to see Kody today, she hadn't fully taken the time to process everything that happened. "Look, I didn't expect you to beat up three kids."

Even though they already discussed it, to her it felt like a good distraction.

"This again?" He called her out on it. But her ploy worked anyway, because he kept going. "Look, I'm your hero. That's what you called me. So when I saw you get pushed down, I had to step up."

"Oh, now you're going to agree to being my hero?" She said aggravated, that he couldn't seem to make up his mind.

He shrugged his shoulders.

"Still, is that what heroes do?" she asked. "Hurt other people?"

"No. Not intentionally anyways. Those are vigilantes. They hurt people to send a message. They're often far more interesting than heroes, because they don't usually have a code of honor." Kody looked down at the floor and stuffed his hands in his pockets. "I never meant to hurt them. I told you that."

His hair was flopped to one side, and he suddenly looked sad. Callie had never seen that look on his face. He was always so upbeat and cheerful.

Now she felt guilty for bringing it up. He was clearly upset about it, and she didn't mean make him feel worse, all because she didn't want to talk about her father's abuse.

"Well, maybe you could find a better way next time. Maybe try talking it out? I don't want you getting hurt. What if you got hurt?"

"Me? Nah, I'm indestructible." He waved off the notion and laughed as though her concerns didn't matter.

"You're *not* indestructible, though," she exclaimed. "Nobody is!" Why didn't he understand? Now he wants to make jokes? She stormed off to her next class, hoping he didn't follow. She brushed past a couple of kids in the hallway.

"Hey watch it!" One boy shouted as he almost dropped his books.

Callie thought maybe Gene would know what was up with Kody. He had always been headstrong, but something about his actions seemed a bit bolder than usual. It was as though he had nothing to lose.

She continued to replay the events at her house over and over in her head. Nothing seemed to make sense anymore. She was not wrong very often, and she knew what she saw.

Maybe she was going crazy, but it was more likely that something strange was going on. Kody was a hard person to get a read on, but she would figure it out. She knew he could be careless and because he didn't pay much attention, it was just a matter of time before the truth came out.

During lunch, Callie saw Gene standing in the corner where their table used to be. He looked awkward, holding his tray of food. She walked over to him.

"No place to sit, huh?"

"It appears that way."

"What about over there?" She pointed at a table with a few empty chairs.

"None of the chairs are next to each other. I'm not comfortable sitting next to someone I don't know." He looked around nervously.

"Well, we could ask someone to slide over and I could sit between you and them." She continued to look.

"Maybe I'll just eat here." Gene set his tray on the window ledge, holding it in place with one hand so it didn't fall.

"Sounds good to me. I'm sure they'll have a new table for us next week." Callie set her lunch bag on the ledge and pulled out an apple.

"Oh, next week will be totally different with Kody back in lunch," Gene said. "Nobody is going to mess with him. He'll be able to sit wherever he wants. And then, so will I." Gene smiled as he stared at his tray.

"Gene, he's not a bully. He isn't going to demand people get up and move." Callie said.

"I suspect he won't have to."

There was a brief moment of silence between them before Callie decided to just take the leap.

"Is something going on with Kody?"

"There's always something going on with Kody. Could you be more specific?" Gene said as he began organizing the food on his tray so it was properly weighted to balance on the ledge of the window.

Callie turned and stared at Gene. "Does he have powers or something?"

This caught Gene off guard, and he carelessly fumbled his tray, sending everything to the floor in a loud crash.

"Powers?" Gene said nervously as he bent down to quickly pick up his mess. "Don't be ridiculous! What would make you say such a thing?" The students in the cafeteria glanced over, but it didn't take long for them to turn back around and go about their business.

Under normal circumstances, Gene probably would have been too embarrassed to move, but he was far too concerned about Callie's suspicion to worry about everyone looking their way.

"Well," she began. "Kody came to visit me, and my dad had been drinking. There was some arguing, and when my dad stumbled, he…" She lowered her voice and looked around. "He accidentally fired his gun. I'm pretty sure he hit Kody, but he seemed fine even after he fell out of the tree."

Gene picked up his tray with everything piled up on it, and looked her straight in the eye. "Clearly if he was fine then he could not have been shot. He's lucky he didn't break anything falling out of the tree. Now, if you'll excuse me, I need to throw this out and, um, go see my academic advisor about setting up my schedule for next year."

Gene hurried off and dumped the entire tray in the garbage on his way out of the cafeteria.

Callie watched him go and took a large bite out of her apple. Something was not right.

The weekend was a welcome reprieve from all the drama that happened at school during the week. Kody had been looking forward to meeting up with Gene. Being invulnerable could have some amazing benefits, and he had so many thoughts running through his head; the conversation with Dean Winters felt like it had happened years ago.

Gene suggested that with 'armor-like' skin, Kody's movements may end up being more restricted if he didn't stay limber. Having been raised by someone who taught Aikido, Kody knew all about stretching; he did it every morning. He discovered at a young age that he was actually very flexible, and his new armor-like skin didn't seem to change that.

Once he was done with his stretches, he checked his phone. No messages. It was like looking in the refrigerator for something to eat and then looking again several minutes later expecting something new to appear.

The disappointment was about the same: it left him empty and unsatisfied.

A knock at the fire-escape door distracted him from his phone. Nobody used that entrance. Kody never had visitors, and even if he did, he would direct them to the back entrance of the Aikido school, which was like their front door. Quietly, Kody approached the door and listened. No sounds. He looked out the peep-hole to see if anyone was there, but all he saw was the building on the other side of the alley.

Kody stepped out onto the fire escape and looked around. Still, there was no one around. Who would be playing games with him today of all days? When he turned to go back into his loft, there was a sealed envelope taped to his door. The envelope was old, stained with dirt and what appeared to be spattered blood. Oddly, the envelope didn't appear to have been tampered with. Whatever adventure this letter had been through, it had not been torn open, and didn't look to have been tampered with at all.

Suspiciously, he pulled the letter off the door, and looked around again to make sure no one was watching him. Knocking on a door to announce their presence and then disappearing like a ghost was a curious way to do things. Whoever left this envelope wanted to remain anonymous. Kody went into his loft and shut the door behind him, locking it. Tearing off one side of the envelope, he pulled out the letter inside.

Kody looked around as if he were in a room full of people he didn't want reading over his shoulder. He slowly unfolded the letter and saw that it was dated nearly 14 years ago. That's when it occurred to him that today was his birthday! When you don't celebrate them, birthdays sneak up on you quickly. Shihan Toshihiro told him that getting older is no reason to celebrate. He usually came through with a cupcake or something from a local bakery or grocery store, but it wasn't something they talked about on a regular basis. There was no build-up, no talk about what presents he wanted. Everything was always very low-key with Shihan. He didn't even get to blow out a candle. It was a cupcake or brownie or something sweet, and it was never accompanied by the words 'Happy Birthday'.

His cell phone buzzed. He pushed the button to silence it. He wanted to read this letter before he got distracted with anything else.

Son,

Son? He read further...

I wish I could have seen you grow into the young man you are today. It has been difficult to stay away all these years, but it was important in order to protect you. I hope you can forgive me for not being there. There are so many things I want to say, but I'm already risking a lot just by sending this to you.

You may be in great danger.

Shihan Toshihiro should have something for you. Contained in this letter is a key. It will unlock the answers you seek. You are destined for great things my son.

I love you,
Dad

PS: A child's legacy lies dormant in his father's sole.

Kody sat and stared at the letter from his father. He

looked in the envelope to see if there was a key was in there. Nothing. Frantically he searched the floor around him to see if a key had fallen out, but his search came up empty.

His phone buzzed again. He ignored it.

Jumping off of his stool, he ran to the old man's door and began banging on it as loudly as he could.

"Shihan Toshihiro! Shihan open up! It's me, Kody!"

The door swung open, and the little man looked up at him. "What going on? You give me heart attack!"

Kody ignored his manners and barged past him. "Close the door!"

Shihan Toshihiro closed the door slowly and reached for the chain lock to slide it in place. Then he turned the deadbolt. After placing a doorstop under the crack, Shihan Toshihiro reached for a chair.

"Seriously?"

"What?" The old man propped the chair against the door handle. "You seem very nervous. Can't be too careful."

"You knew my father and never told me?"

"Who say I knew your father?"

"Who *say* you didn't?" Kody waved the letter in the air. "I just got a letter. *From him!* It was on my door this morning with no return address. It says you have something for me?"

Shihan Toshihiro waddled over to Kody, using his cane for support with each step. "Let me see." He snatched the letter from Kody and began reading.

Waiting impatiently, Kody began pacing back and forth.

"Is joke," the old man said dismissively. "Someone play mean trick on you. Very mean. No funny at all." He tucked the letter into his robe.

"Come on, Shihan, don't mess with me. I'm serious here. *This* is serious! Did my dad leave you in charge of taking care of me?"

"No, no, no, no." The old man said as he made his way over to his fireplace. "Everything I tell you is true. Your mother she…she vanish, and leave you here with me. Shihan Toshihiro teach Kody. Raise Kody."

"Yeah, you told me that. You also said you knew nothing about my father. According to that letter, it sounds like you also *lied* to Kody."

"I no lie; is dishonorable. Leave parts out maybe; not as dishonorable," he said with a wry smile.

"You're going to tell me everything you know!" Kody clenched his fists. If there was ever a time he could stay focused on the old man's gibberish, it was right now.

"Tell you everything? No, that take far too long. How about I tell some things. Important things." The old man waddled over to his fireplace and tapped on the bricks underneath the vent. "Start here."

Kody approached the fireplace and knelt down in front of it. "Tell me what you know about my parents. Like, how did you know them?"

Shihan sat down in the rocking chair by the fireplace and pointed. "If Kody want truth, Kody need to start digging."

The old man leaned his head back and chuckled a bit. "Start digging, that very funny."

Kody looked up at the brick Shihan had tapped. Reaching out to it, he felt it wiggle. He grabbed at it, and slowly worked it away from the hearth until it came out. Then he pulled out another one. And another. He kept going until he had a stack of bricks in front of him. When it seemed he had removed all of the ones that were loose, Kody reached up into the opening he created. He felt a handle and pulled on it carefully.

A dusty old briefcase slid down into his hands. A pair of dusty old boots tumbled out after it, falling to the ground and kicking up some ash.

"Uh, that's a weird place to keep a pair of boots."

Moving the items to the coffee table, Kody gently set them down and stared at the strange pairing of items. "What does it mean?"

"*Big* trouble," Shihan answered.

Kody inspected the dusty old charcoal combat boots. There didn't seem to be anything special about them.

"Those were father's boots." Shihan said as he sat still in his chair, eyes closed.

Kody slid off his sneakers and tried the boots on. Surprisingly, they fit! "Well, they aren't new, but they're new to me," he said. "Now for the briefcase."

He reached over and popped the latches to open it up. Inside were a bunch of documents, full of formulas, that made no sense to him. There were a few letters, and some pictures of his mom holding him when he was just a baby.

In one picture that caught his attention, there was a man sitting in a chair, with his back to the camera.

"Is that...my dad?"

Shihan Toshihiro nodded.

"Why didn't you tell me that you knew my dad!"

"Less you know, the better." Shihan stood up, "Come, time to open dojo."

"That letter said there was a key." Kody said closing up

the briefcase. "I didn't see any key." He stood up and followed the old man downstairs.

The picture wasn't much, but it was the only time he had ever seen any evidence of his father. All this time growing up, it was like his father wasn't even a real person, until now. He was the only one who ever talked about him, because no one in Kody's life ever claimed to have known him.

At least that's what he had been led to believe.

His mother had disappeared when he was too young to remember. All he knew is that Shihan Toshihiro got sad anytime she was mentioned. Kody had no knowledge of his past. Nothing to link him to his parents.

Until now.

"You need to come clean and tell me everything you know," Kody demanded as they descended the stairwell. "About my dad. About my mom. How did my parents meet? I always assumed my dad didn't know I existed. What's his name? Where did my mom disappear to? Have you been keeping that from me too? Why all th-?"

The old man stopped in his tracks and held his hand up quickly, cutting off the questioning. Kody almost ran into him, but caught himself. The two stood silently in the hallway for a moment, listening.

Kody heard something in the dojo.

Several somethings.

Shihan Toshihiro whispered, "We have company."

They walked out onto the floor to see five men dressed in white from head to toe, their masks revealing only their eyes. They were rummaging through files, cabinets, and drawers near the front desk.

A sixth man stood by watching his men wreck the place. He was dressed in similar fashion, only his clothing was all dark red. His face was wrapped in bandages, stained with blood.

When Kody and Shihan appeared, all of them stopped what they were doing and looked up.

The man in red pointed at Kody. "He has the briefcase!" His voice was raspy and sent a chill down Kody's spine.

Kody looked down at the old leather case and held it

behind his back. What did they know about the briefcase?

"Get them!" The short, bandaged man commanded.

As the men in white charged, Shihan leaned his cane against the wall and held his arms out to his sides. As each attacker approached, one-by-one, the little old man grabbed at their arms. By using carefully placed grips on their wrists and elbows, he twisted his body, effortlessly, to send them flailing to the ground in all directions. Then he grabbed up the cane and used it to swipe the briefcase from Kody's hands, creeping across the dojo floor with the gentle grace of a cat.

The briefcase was now in his care.

Kody moved to get between Shihan Toshihiro and the men getting back to their feet. He held his arms out at the ready.

"Forget the boy! The briefcase is what matters." The bandaged man stood there shouting his commands. Kody looked at him long enough for three of the five men to get around him. He recovered in time to trip the fourth and grab the arm of the fifth.

Spinning his body, while twisting the man's arm at the elbow, he watched as the attacker flipped onto the ground in pain. Just like in his training. It was hard to believe it required so little effort to send a grown man to the floor, but the manipulation of the joint causes so much pain the attacker became a puppet, moving where and how Kody wanted him to.

He looked over his shoulder to see Shihan Toshihiro toying with the other three. They'd get up, and they'd go right back down. Without throwing a single punch, the old man moved around the floor, tossing them all aside like ragdolls. He wasted very little energy doing so, while still maintaining control of the briefcase.

The two men Kody dropped to the floor stood back up and attacked him at the same time. He sidestepped to his right and reached for his attacker's forearm, sending a palm-strike into the man's rib cage, followed by a push-kick into the attacker's body. This sent the intruder into the other, and both stumbled and fell over each other.

"ENOUGH!" The bandaged man clapped his hands once and the attackers immediately retreated, forming up behind him. "You will turn over the briefcase and all the documents inside at once."

"Have better idea," Shihan Toshihiro replied defiantly. "You will leave my dojo and never return."

"You haven't heard the last of me, old man. I will get that briefcase. I don't care if I have to pry it from your cold, dead hands."

"If you don't care," Kody said, "we'll take the option that's not that one." Kody wanted to tell them to get out, but as he opened his mouth, he saw his mentor's hand go up, as if to stop him from speaking. It worked. He was probably going to make a fool of himself anyways.

"We know who you are." The short, unimposing man said. We will find anyone that means anything to you, and destroy all that you hold dear until you crumble. When we're through, you will *beg* me to take that briefcase off of your hands, just to salvage what's left of your pathetic existence."

"Wait!" The interjection just leaped from Kody's mouth. "So, you aren't going to kill us for it? I'm confused, because first you said you were going to kill us, and now your threatening to kill other people."

"I'll do both."

"Will you though? It doesn't sound like you've thought this through very well. Are you new to this sort of thing?"

The bandaged man reached into his belt, pulled out a pellet and threw it at Kody's feet. "You haven't heard the last of us!" he shouted. The pellet exploded and filled the room with black smoke.

Kody gagged and coughed as he scrambled to escape for clean air. "Friggin' pajama wearing ninjas!" he managed to say between coughs.

When the smoke cleared, Kody began looking around on the floor.

"What Kody doing?"

"Checking to see if they dropped any coins?"

"This not a video game!" Shihan Toshihiro yelled and jabbed at the floor with his cane.

"Ugh. Real life is so stupid." Kody looked up at the old man. "Wait, why are you opening the door?"

"Because," Shihan Toshihiro said in perfect English, without the slightest hint of an accent. "It is time to clear the air."

Kody looked at his master and caregiver, stunned at what he was hearing. "Are you pulling my leg? How long have you been able to talk like that?"

"Always," he replied. "But when I was asked to raise you in secrecy, I felt that pretending to be a crazy old Asian dude with broken English was a good cover. It seemed to work. But now that things are beginning to unravel, there's no reason to pretend around you anymore."

Kody gripped at his hair with both hands. His mind was blown. "What's beginning to unravel?"

"The truth," Shihan Toshihiro said, "I am your-"

"Father?!"

"No, I'm your *grand*-father. And it's time for your real

training to begin." Graceful as a cat and quick as a snake, Shihan Toshihiro moved in and flipped Kody to the ground.

Kody stared up at the old man. "You've got to be kidding me."

"My daughter, your mother, Sumiko, moved to America to study at Johns Hopkins University, where she met your father, Doctor Eric Haywood."

"Wait," Kody said, "You told me that my mom's name was Sue. Oh, I get it."

The old man helped Kody to his feet. "Before you were born, your mother was concerned about Eric's dealings," he said. "She asked that I come to watch over the family. After your father left, I helped raise you boys as a foolish old immigrant, to avoid drawing too much attention to us. Daniel always knew I was your grandfather, but he picked on you so much, getting him to play along was easy. And then, one day, your mother was gone too. Vanished without a trace."

Kody looked at the sadness that drew over the old man's face. He took the opportunity to strike, hoping to catch his grandfather off guard, but he was quickly turned around and flipped to the mat.

"Why did she leave? Did she tell you?" Kody threw a flurry of punches, all easily blocked.

"Her heart was broken!" He stepped under a jab and slid his leg forward and behind his student. A slight push with his arm outstretched, once again sent the younger, stronger boy to the floor. "She was lost, and spiraled into a deep depression. I came home one day to find you here. Alone. With no note. Nothing." Tears filled the man's eyes as though he were feeling the pain all over again for the first time.

"Shihan, I-" Kody said.

"No!" The man turned away. "What's done is done. My daughter is no longer with us, and your father is clearly a madman. Corrupted. His research must have put her in danger, and now you. These men, they want your father's research."

"Well, they aren't going to get it unless they answer some questions. Like, what does it all mean?" Kody's face twisted. "Wait a minute." His eyes looked over at the far wall, which held several swords. Then he looked at the briefcase, as a realization dawned on him. "You've got to be kidding me." Kody walked across the room and took a sword down from the wall.

"What are you doing?" Shihan Toshihiro asked.

"Something happened to me the other day," Kody said. "Something that didn't make any sense until this briefcase turned up full of stuff that I can't make heads or tails of. Then a bunch of ninjas pop into the dojo, thinking they're hot stuff, and try taking the briefcase." Kody pulled the sword from its sheath.

"Kody!"

He raised the sword in the air and held out his left arm. "What did my father do?" He asked.

"You don't understand what you're doing."

"Really? Tell me what I don't understand! That the one person I was supposed to trust lied to me about my parents? That you've kept a secret from me that I was bound to find out about? I bet my name's not even Kody!"

Shihan Toshihiro shrugged. "Ehhhh, it is, mostly."

"Oh, come on!" Kody yelled in frustration. He slammed the blade down onto his forearm. The sword shattered against his skin, sending shards of metal raining to the floor. "You see that? I'm a science experiment!"

Shihan Toshihiro rushed to Kody's side and grabbed his arm. He stared in astonishment. "This cannot be. Not even a scratch."

"Yeah. I have literally been shot *and* hit by a car. Not even a scratch." Kody echoed.

Shihan contemplated the unscathed arm, the bits of sword at his feet.

"Ko."

"What?"

"Your mother wanted a Japanese name for you," Shihan said. "Ko means 'peace.' Your father wanted something more American sounding. So, they agreed on Kody. But your mother always called you Ko." He picked up the briefcase. "This must contain all the research needed to understand your gift. It makes sense why they want it now. Think of what could happen if they sold this to the wrong people? Someone could create an army of indestructible soldiers."

"Bulletproof ones."

"Or worse." The color left Shihan Toshihiro's face. "Bomb-proof."

Kody was no stranger to the news. Suicide bombers wreaked havoc on public places overseas. He couldn't imagine what went through someone's head to do something like that, to have a mission that wasn't successful unless you died. But with the ability to withstand a blast like that, there would be no death for the bomber. It would be detonate, kill, and repeat.

They could manufacture an army of human weapons.

"Alright," Kody said. "Let's start training. Next time they show up, I want to be ready. This is *my* gift, and I refuse to let someone else unwrap it." Kody raised his eyebrows, hoping for approval.

Shihan shook his head. "Weak attempts at humor will not help you win in battle."

As the two talked inside the dojo, a vintage red Plymouth Barracuda with black racing stripes pulled up outside the open door of the studio. The black-tinted windows were rolled up, muffling the sound of heavy metal music, but just barely. The sound was ear piercing.

It became impossibly louder when the car door opened, and Kody's older brother, Dan, stepped out of the car. He said something lost to the din of the metal, and Kody shrugged his shoulders and shook his head.

Dan rolled his eyes and leaned into the car to shut the music off. "Happy birthday, little bro!" He walked into the studio with his arms outstretched, and gave Kody a strong, suffocating hug.

Kody had forgotten how big of a man his brother was. Muscles bulged through his black polo shirt, and veins popped from his forearms. It was hard to believe they were related in any way, and because they didn't talk much, sometimes it was easy for Kody to forget he even had a brother. Dan usually only called when he needed something.

Kody wondered what he needed this time.

He picked up the briefcase and approached the vehicle. "Where did you get that car?" It was beautiful. It had to have cost his brother a lot of money and, last he knew, his brother was struggling to make ends meet.

"Let's just say I closed a shrewd business deal and made out like a bandit." Dan ran his hand across the hood in admiration of his toy. "So, you want to go for a ride on your birthday?"

It wasn't the best time to be cruising around town, but Kody found himself wanting to spend time with his brother. He almost never saw him, and he wanted to have a relationship with him. Every year, Dan would visit for Kody's birthday, but spend the entire time complaining about being broke and talking about how someday he would get his big break.

One year, Dan had come to him begging for money. He was going to the casino to play blackjack and had a surefire plan to strike it rich. He had read somewhere that you could count cards and play the percentages. Kody, always wanting to help, took most of his savings out of the bank and gave it to him. He was family, after all, and any chance Kody could help, he would.

This time it seemed Dan was finally doing well for himself. And while the words 'shrewd business deal' coming from his brother's mouth made his skin crawl, this birthday hangout seemed pretty harmless. Dan didn't ask for anything, he just wanted to spend time together. Kody felt like he could use a healthy distraction, and going for a ride and talking with his brother would be good for him.

Kody looked to Shihan who waved him off. "Go. Have fun. And be careful." The thick accent had returned, which concerned Kody. Did Shihan not trust Dan?

"Alright, old man says go! You ready scamp?" Dan said, pulling his sunglasses down his nose so he could see Kody better. "Did you grow? You seem, taller."

"A little bit I suppose." Kody slid into the passenger seat of the car, and frowned at the strong smell of coconut. Five air freshener trees hung from the rearview mirror. "This car is—" he stifled a gag "—awesome bro."

"Thanks!" Dan revved up the engine and shifted it into gear before Kody could get his seatbelt on. As soon as Kody's belt clicked into place, Dan shifted gears again, and stepped on the gas pedal.

SCREEEEEEECH!!

The tires screamed as they spun against the pavement. Smoke filled the air as they took off down the street.

Kody swallowed hard and grabbed his seat. "So, where are we headed?"

"I got a little surprise for you for your birthday! You'll see when we get there."

Dan drove like a maniac heading deep into the city, zipping down main roads, back roads and side streets until Kody had no clue where he was. He had been turned around so many times, he had no way of telling where they were anymore. Staying close to home and riding his skateboard suddenly had significant disadvantages. Dan blasted the heavy metal music and didn't say a word.

Kody began to get concerned.

He thought he was just going to go for a ride with his brother, and they would talk about things: School, sports, graduation, girls, or anything else brothers might talk about. Of course, his brother never showed interest in bonding with him before, so he felt like a fool for thinking today was any different.

Looking around, Kody decided they were somewhere in a bad part of the city. There was garbage lying in the road, a few folks in tattered clothes sitting on the sidewalks. Of the few people out walking, none of them walked alone.

They pulled into an alley between two buildings, and Dan slowed down as he approached a metal garage door. He honked the horn three times, and the door opened slowly. They drove inside, and there were several more cars like Dan's.

"Dan, where are we?" Kody's eyes widened. Was Dan getting him a car?

Dan parked the car in a spot next to a green car, another muscle car. Kody wasn't sure of the make or model, but it looked like modifications had been made to it.

"Come on, let's go, scamp." When Dan hopped out of the car, Kody realized his brother had never even buckled up.

"You should really wear your seat belt," Kody said as he got out. "The way you drive, it would be safer in case you get into an accident."

"I'm really not that concerned about it, little brother." Dan took off his sunglasses and tucked them into his shirt collar. He stopped in the middle of the garage and put his hands in his jeans pockets as he looked around.

"Umm what are we doing here?" Kody was starting to get concerned. Something didn't seem right. He didn't care how relaxed Dan appeared.

"There's a friend of mine that wants to meet you," Dan replied. A door opened under a lit exit sign, and a man dressed in a suit, wearing black leather gloves and holding a suitcase, came walking out. "Ah, here he is now."

Kody tucked his hands into the pockets of his hoodie. Shivers coursed through his whole body as the man approached them. He did not like what was happening, and he felt very uneasy. He trusted his brother, but it was all very strange to him. "Dan?"

"Relax scamp, he just wants to meet you." Kody noticed Dan's hands were out of his pockets now and he was rubbing his fingers together.

The stranger approached Dan and glanced at Kody with dark inset eyes. "This is him? Your brother?" His thick accent caused Kody's heart to jump.

"Yeah, this is him. Is that for me?" Dan looked at the suitcase, his fingers still rubbing together.

The man smiled and laughed, "Yes, this is for you." The suitcase exchanged hands and the stranger smiled at Kody, clenching his gloved hands into fists.

Kody watched in awe as his brother popped open the suitcase. He smiled big and then shut it tight, latching it back up. "Pleasure doing business with you," Dan said and then turned to Kody. "Look scamp, you'll understand when your older." Dan opened his car door, tossed the briefcase inside and climbed in.

"Wait!" Kody yelled at him and ran to the passenger door.

It was locked.

Kody banged on the window with his fists. "Open the door! Come on Dan, you can't do this to me!"

Dan backed up the car, and Kody jumped out of the way, watching helplessly as his older brother drove off.

Kody couldn't understand why his brother would do this to him. Betrayed by his brother for money? The stranger stood still and stared at him. The only sound came from the heavy metal garage door closing.

"You will come with me." The man said, "I have someone interested in meeting you." His accent was thick, making it hard for Kody to understand him. He held his hand out, inviting Kody to walk in the direction of an access door.

Stalling for time, Kody asked, "Who are you?" He wasn't sure what he planned to do with the time, but he wasn't ready to go anywhere with this stranger. "Are you with those pajama wearing fools that tried attacking me earlier?"

"I am no one of consequence," he replied. "However, I can tell you that you would be wise to cooperate. The Khan has a great number of questions for you."

"If he has questions then he can come to me." Kody tried to be stern but then he smirked. "I mean, you're trying to abduct me and you don't even offer me some candy? Where's the windowless van? What is this, your first gig?"

"I am not in the mood for your games." The stranger began slowly approaching Kody. "Walk with me, or be dragged by me, it does not matter."

"That's close enough!" Kody said while holding out his hands in protest, but the stranger kept walking, "Back off!" he demanded.

The man pulled a gun out of his suit jacket and yanked the slide back, putting one in the chamber; aiming it at Kody. At that moment, Kody realized this stranger didn't understand what was going on. He was just an errand boy doing what he was told.

If he'd had any information, he would know that a gun wouldn't be enough.

Whoever was after his father's research was wealthy enough to get hired help--including Dan! They weren't brave enough to do it themselves, though, and that gave Kody the upper hand. It also explained why his father was able to be so elusive; he had clearly outsmarted them the whole way.

Kody wasn't going to outsmart anyone. He would have to fight his way out.

He put his hands up in a defensive position as though he were going to submit.

The man walked around behind him. "Good," he said. "Start walking. There is no time to waste."

As soon as Kody felt the gun poke him in the back, he spun around and sent a backfist into the man's head.

THWAP!

BANG!

The gun fired, and Kody felt the bullet hit his shoulder, tearing his hoodie, but bouncing off of him.

His attacker was hurt, but not down. His glasses had been shattered, and his eye was swollen and bleeding. Disregarding the fact that Kody just took a bullet without injury, the man fired directly into Kody's chest.

BANG! BANG! BANG!

Kody staggered back from the force of the bullets hitting him. A look of fear drew across the stranger's face as Kody shrugged his shoulders and smiled. "What are those, blanks?" he said teasingly. "Doesn't your boss trust you with the big boy bullets?"

Angrily, the man threw his weapon at Kody.

Ducking out of the way, Kody looked at the stranger in disgust. "Really?"

The strange henchman attacked with a flurry of punches. This wasn't a kid from high school attacking him, or a bunch of grown men in ninja pajamas. This was a trained killer, and

Kody had no one to back him up this time.

He stepped backward with his arms up defensively. His attacker was relentless, and while the blows weren't hurting him, they were a nuisance.

Punches continued to rain down on him. Kody couldn't be sure, but he thought he took several blows to the body that may have been from kicks. He was confused by how quickly this man moved, and he wasn't sure what to do. He kept moving backward, absorbing each blow as though someone were beating him back with a pillow.

Suddenly, Kody's back bumped into something and he could no longer retreat. Feeling the cold concrete behind him, Kody reached out in spite of the attacks, and grabbed the man by his suit jacket. Spinning around, he thrust the man into the support beam behind him, face first.

POP!

The impact of the man's head cracked the beam, flaking off a few chunks of concrete, sending him slumping to the floor unconscious.

Kody stood still for a few moments, not sure what to do next. It was eerily quiet in the parking garage, and although he knew he needed to get home, he wasn't entirely sure where he was. He had never felt so alone in his life.

He had grown up without a father, who is now sending him letters from the grave. His mother had disappeared when he was very young. His brother had just tried selling him.

His phone buzzed in his pocket. Reluctantly, he pulled it out and looked to see who was calling him. It was Gene.

"Hey," Kody said.

His friend's reply was frantic. "Where are you?"

"I'm..." Kody sat in silence for a moment as the day's events washed over him. He stared at the garage exit, unable to move his feet. Finally, he choked back a few tears and replied.

"I'm lost."

As much as he would have loved to confront his older brother, Kody had a feeling that, since he didn't stick around, and the buyer was left empty handed, Dan would be a hard man to find. His buyers would be looking to get their money back.

Kody didn't even care. A small part of him hoped The Khan's men caught up with his older brother. Maybe that would teach him a lesson.

After Gene had calmed him down over the phone, Kody left the parking garage and walked several blocks before finding a taxi to take him home. He needed to get the briefcase and the mysterious letter to Gene. He was the only person Kody could trust right now with everything else going on.

When Kody arrived at Gene's late that night, Gene was alone. Gene's parents were almost never home. It was because of their frequent absences that he had been able to accomplish so much at such a young age. Having two parents that traveled for work, and with him having been far more mature than most kids his age, Gene learned early on how to take care of himself.

The boy spent nearly all of his time learning and researching, inventing and experimenting. Some of the greatest scientific minds on the planet had gotten paid a lot of money for what Gene considered 'a hobby'.

"Wait," the boy genius said. "Your brother tried selling you? That's insane!"

"Yes," Kody responded in the most serious tone Gene had ever heard come from his mouth. "That's why I'm here. Some guy named 'The Khan' wants me for some reason."

"Well, we know the reason."

"You know what I mean. Anyway, before that happened, we got attacked at the dojo by some pajama-wearing dudes."

"Sounds like you've had a busy day."

Kody set the briefcase on one of Gene's tables. "Ninety percent of what we need to know is in here," he said indicating the case. "The other half is a riddle. I think."

"You're a riddle." Gene fired back, fighting the urge to correct Kody's math, again.

"Gene, look at this letter." Kody pulled the folded-up piece of paper from his pocket and held it out.

Gene took it and opened it up. Reading the letter, his eyes widened with each word. "This isn't some kind of prank is it?"

"It arrived on my doorstep."

"Your doorstep is a fire escape."

Kody raised his eyebrows, silently indicating that was his point.

Gene read the letter again and frowned. "He spelled

'soul' incorrectly."

"That's what you got from this?" Kody asked. "Bad spelling? Gene, the man is literally speaking to me from the grave with this letter."

Gene continued to examine the letter, turning it over and back again. "The degradation of the paper appears to be appropriate for a letter this old. The handwriting doesn't seem forced or fabricated."

Sitting down in his chair, the boy genius turned on a purple light, holding the paper underneath it.

"Don't ruin it."

"I won't. I'm just scanning it under a UV light to determine if there is anything hidden to the naked eye; finger-prints and such."

Gene frowned as, after several minutes, nothing appeared. If Kody's father truly did write this letter, he took great care to eliminate any residual evidence.

"Gene," Kody broke the silence. "Everything in this briefcase is what Shihan Toshihiro and I got attacked for. All they wanted was this stuff inside."

"Is Shihan Toshihiro...?"

"He's fine," Kody assured him. "And he knows everything. Oh, and also, he's apparently my grandfather!"

Gene's jaw dropped.

"Yeah, Gene, he kept that information from me this whole time. And he knew about my parents, and said it's time for my 'real training' to start."

"And the ninjas?"

"They said that they'd be back, and they were going to hurt the people we care about. Or kill us. Or both." Kody replayed the threats in his head. "I think they were a little confused, honestly. Either way, they want this briefcase, and they don't care who they have to go through to get it." Kody flopped into an empty chair. He leaned forward and buried his head in his hands, pushing his thick, black hair back on his head.

Gene stood up, "I might have something that will put a

smile on your face." He went over to a shelf and pulled out an object wrapped in a sheet, handing it to Kody.

"What's this?"

"It's your birthday gift. I've been working on it for quite some time."

Kody set the long, thin, and light object on his lap and pulled the sheet off of it, revealing the platform of a skateboard missing its wheels.

His jaw dropped.

"Is this what I think it is?" he exclaimed. "Because it looks like what I think it is! It's like a science fiction dream come true!"

"More like science *fact* my friend." Gene smiled with confidence. "It's been tested and it works. Go ahead, hop on."

Kody set the board on the ground and stood on it. "How do I…?"

Gene tapped a metal plate on the board. The board hummed, then lifted off the ground. Kody struggled to keep his balance as the board hovered in place. It took him a moment to acclimate to being off the ground, but it did not take him long before he leveled out and remained still.

"I have my very own hoverboard!" Kody pulled his phone out of his pocket, stuck out his tongue, and took a selfie. His pre-paid phone didn't have the best camera, but he worked with what he had. Putting the phone away, he leaned forward and the board moved with him, slowly. Then he leaned back and it slowed to a stop.

"I'm not going to explain the science behind how it works because it's all over your head anyways," Gene said. "But trust when I tell you, it's a one-of-a-kind piece of hardware. *Do not break it!*"

As though fate was listening, Kody lost his balance and landed on his hip. The board shot towards the brick wall in front of him.

"Oops." He went over to inspect the damage, but it seemed unscratched.

"Oh, right," Gene chuckled. "I almost forgot. It's not *going* to break. I made it virtually Kody-proof." He paused to laugh even harder. "It's constructed with a titanium-steel alloy shell, with a thin layer of highly absorbent, impact resistant gel surrounding the important electronics inside. That being said, you'll need slightly magnetized metal inserts in your shoes in order to maintain contact with the board."

"Wait, you want to modify the boots?" Kody asked. "You aren't going to ruin them, are you? These were my dad's boots. They fell out of the fireplace."

"The fireplace?" Gene exclaimed. "You know what? I'm not even going to ask. At this point, nothing should surprise me." Gene opened a drawer and pulled out two thin sheets of metal. Each sheet had a honeycomb pattern on both sides. "Let me see your boots. I'll install them quickly, and then you can take it for a test drive on the open road."

Gene made quick work of installing the first magnet. He cut into the sole of the boot and slid the insert inside the rubber.

When he cut into the second boot, there was a surprise waiting inside.

A piece of metal popped out and onto the floor.

"What is that?" Kody asked, picking it up.

Gene scooped up the letter from Kody's dad and read out loud. *"The key to a child's legacy lies dormant in his father's sole."* Gene looked at the boot and then at the piece of metal. "Is there anything on that?"

"Just a bunch of numbers."

"Kody, that's the key. The 'sole' wasn't a spelling error, it meant the sole of your father's boot! It was meant to be a clue!"

Gene snatched the key from Kody's hand to inspect it closer. It had a logo—IBoPH—on the opposite side of the numbers. "This is for the International Bank of Port Haven. Your father must have a safe deposit box stored there."

Kody looked up at the ceiling. "What the heck dad?" He spoke as if the ghost of his father was haunting him. He looked at Gene. "So, what do you think this means?"

"It means on Monday, when the Emerging Leaders program heads downtown after school, I'm going with you and we're sneaking off to the bank."

Kody's smile returned.

The next day, Kody and Gene met up and took a bus downtown to give the hoverboard a test run. Gene had given Kody a trench coat, and a bandolier to wear under it.

"I'm not wearing that," he protested the bulky trench coat.

"And why not?" Gene asked. "It's very practical for hiding things."

"Yeah but, it's not a cape," said Kody. "I always dreamed that if I was going to be a superhero, I'd have a cape. Superheroes have capes, dude!"

"Statistically speaking," Gene replied, pushing his glasses up on his nose, "a very small number of heroes wear capes. It shouldn't even qualify as a cliché."

"Yeah, but the ones who do are usually the best." As disappointed as Kody was, he knew arguing would get him nowhere. There was a high-powered magnet on the back of the bandolier that Kody could attach the hoverboard to; the trench coat was meant to hide it.

The bandolier went over his left shoulder and attached to his belt. Two more straps extended across his body, one going around his ribcage and the other going over his right shoulder. Both connected to the back magnet, keeping the entire unit secure.

It forced Kody to stand up on the bus, but it was worth it knowing he would take his board out for a test spin downtown.

When they arrived at the bus station, the two friends got off and started walking the two blocks toward the harbor. They could smell the salt in the air. The early morning fog was thick, and low enough that it reduced visibility.

"The fog will reduce our chances of being seen," Gene said. "But just in case, put this on."

Kody examined the thing Gene handed him. "Is this a mask?"

"Is that concern or enthusiasm?"

"Can it be both?" Kody said with a smile.

"I suppose it can be," Gene replied. "Put it on and let me know how it fits."

Kody fitted the mask over his face. The visor wrapped around his head and rested on his ears. The lenses were white from the outside, yet he could somehow see everything in high definition from behind them. Attached to the visor was a faceplate that covered his nose and mouth. There were holes around the faceplate, six evenly placed in a circle surrounding a seventh hole.

Gene smiled. "The visor is equipped with a heads-up display. You aren't actually looking through anything. It's like a high-definition TV monitor underneath."

"This is so cool. Whoa, my voice!" Kody heard a high pitched, synthesized voice when he spoke. He grabbed at his throat; he sounded like a robotic elf.

"Sorry!" Gene said in a panic, "That still needed to be calibrated. I didn't realize it would make your voice so high pitched." He pulled a tool from his satchel and made some adjustments. "It should be a lower frequency now. How's that?"

"You tell me." His voice sounded much, much cooler that time. It was deep and ominous and sounded like he swallowed a pound of gravel. "This is soooooo cool!" He put his hoodie up to cover the rest of his head. "*In a world…*"

"Nope," Gene said. "We're not doing that."

"*Remember, who you are.*"

"Can you be serious for two minutes?"

"*I am your-*"

"'—favorite person in the whole world, I know! Now, can we get on with this?!"

Kody smiled under the mask. He took off the trench coat, revealing the hoverboard clinging to the magnetized bandolier. He held the coat out for his friend to take.

"You'll want to put the coat back on." Gene said.

"Why? Won't it get snagged on something?"

"Not if you're careful," he said. "Look, if you're going to cruise around the city on a hoverboard, people are going to get freaked out. We can't have anyone recognizing you by face or body type, or we're going to get in serious trouble." Gene held up the hooded coat. "This will disguise your body type; it covers you from neck to ankle. Besides, that bandolier is proprietary. I don't want anyone getting a good look at it and stealing the design."

"No one is going to steal your property design."

"Pro-pry-eh-tare-ee." Gene sounded the word out slowly.

"That's not how you say 'property,'" Kody said as he slipped the coat back on.

"I wasn't trying to—" Gene started to correct Kody, but then he realized there was no point to it. "You know what?

Never mind, just get on the board and let's see how you do."

Kody tossed the hoverboard on the ground. It bounced off of nothing and floated six inches above the pavement. He gave the back end of it a nudge, and it moved effortlessly with a gentle spin. Kody's eyes widened as he was eager to get on it.

Adjusting the overcoat on his shoulders he took a moment to look himself over. The fingerless gloves, the mask—it all came together as a complete costume.

Kody was ready.

Nobody would ever recognize him. Which was good, because, while he always dreamed of being a superhero, he was starting to feel a little awkward.

"Wait," he said, reflecting on the moment. "When in the world did you have time to make me a bandolier and a voice synthesizing mask with a built-in, heads-up display?"

"I'd rather not go through a montage of explanations about what I do in my spare time. And besides," Gene put in an earpiece. *"That's not all I built."*

"Whoa!" Kody exclaimed, as Gene's voice came through speakers built into the mask. "Dude I can hear you in my ears!"

Kody hopped onto the hoverboard, flapping his arms to keep his balance. He steadied himself, then wobbled a bit before regaining his balance. "It's like I'm on ice or something."

"There's no friction, only drag." Gene reached into his satchel and pulled out a tablet. Holding it up, he said, "I can track your whereabouts on this device and communicate with you. This will allow you to go anywhere in the city without getting lost."

"That's really smart."

"I know."

Kody bounced up and down on the board, then slowly eased into it, leaning forward. He hovered across the ground, his trench coat flapping behind him. It was like a flying skateboard and making turns proved to be just as easy. He dropped his weight down and jumped up to do a kickflip, but the magnets kept the board from leaving his feet.

He lost his balance and flew into a stack of shipping crates leaning against a nearby building. "How do I disengage the magnets?" he asked.

"I don't advise doing that just so you can do stunts. This is a highly sophisticated piece of equipment," Gene said. "I'd rather it not be broken the first time you use it."

"What? You said it can't be broken! And who said anything about doing stunts?"

"As if you needed to."

"Okay, but," Kody protested, "what if I need to, you know, get off the hoverboard?"

Gene thought for a moment and realized that would have to come up eventually. "There are sensors on the top of the board on either side of your feet. Point your back foot towards the rear of the board, and the magnets will disengage. Once your feet come back in contact with the board, the magnets will connect again."

"Sweet." At this point, Kody had already dusted himself off and was back on the board. Following Gene's instructions, he attempted the kick-flip again.

It worked! When he came down, he wobbled a bit to regain his balance, but he didn't fall. He leaned forward for speed, shooting down the alleyway and racing off into the city.

For the next hour, Kody weaved in and out of traffic, hopping over pedestrian benches and, when the traffic was clear enough, he used the buildings as half-pipes, going up and down either side of them. Some people swore at him as he whipped by, others pointed in awe. Dogs barked, kids clapped, and police officers yelled.

Nobody knew who he was. Kody felt free and his mind was clear.

He had focus.

"As the hours slipped away, darkness slowly consumed daylight…"

"*Hello?*"

"…It came like a hungry beast, devouring the blue sky and any clouds that lay in its path…"

"*Is this thing on?*"

"He crouched on the rooftop, waiting to pounce on the first sign of trouble like a cat…"

"*Kody.*"

"…No, wait. Like a tiger!"

"*KODY!*"

"Yes, Gene?"

"*I don't think it's necessary to provide your own narrative. No one can hear you but me.*" Gene sat in a chair in his parents' wine cellar, manning the control panel.

"Yeah, but the voice synthesizer is just too cool. I could listen to myself talk all day." Kody replied from his perch.

"*I shouldn't have recalibrated it. If you still sounded like an elf, you'd be less likely to carry on like you are,*" Gene said out of frustration.

"No, you should have given me goggles that have x-ray vision," Kody said. "That way I could see if there are crimes happening inside the buildings."

"*I will not condone the use of x-ray vision,*" Gene argued. "*That is a violation of people's privacy. Not to mention you are not mature enough to use them properly.*"

Kody just shrugged his shoulders.

They agreed it would be a good idea for Kody to hang around the city and try to break up a crime. Not that he could arrest anyone; but if they stopped a crime in progress and gave a criminal something to think about, it would be as good as a success. They wanted to establish a good reputation, so starting small would be ideal. Stopping someone snatching a purse would be good, but they weren't above trying to stop a robbery at gunpoint, either. That would really put his abilities on display.

Kody was bored waiting for bad things to happen. He always heard stuff on the news about crime, but now that he was out looking for it, there seemed to be none. "Do you think we should make an official announcement that there's a new hero in town? You know, contact the press?"

"*No,*" Gene said, "*Let your mythology grow organically. Besides, you don't even have a name yet.*"

Kody sat down on the rooftop ledge, kicking his feet against the side of the building while looking out over Port Haven. "Any sign of trouble?" he asked, hopefully.

Suddenly the police scanner stopped on a channel and a request for backup came.

"*...observing a potential conflict, may need backup.*"

"*Unit 9-Zulu-9 what's your 10-20?*"

"Steel Harbor, Dock 22. Lot of people assembling. Looks like several gang factions converging."

Gene's voice cut into the transmission which was simulcast into Kody's mask. *"Are you hearing this?"*

"Yeah, we totally need to be there!" Kody jumped up from his spot on the roof and looked over the edge for a good place to land.

"No, you *need to be there,* Gene corrected. *"I need to stay safe in my chair here at home."*

"How come in cartoons there's always an overhang or produce stand to bounce off of?" Kody asked. "I don't see anything soft to land on." Kody complained as he pulled his hoverboard from the bandolier under his coat.

"Would you stop complaining and get moving? You have a highly sophisticated hoverboard. Treat the building like a half-pipe. I have the best route to the docks, let me know when you are on the ground and mobile."

Kody placed the board under his feet as he leaped from the rooftop. Plummeting five stories to the ground, he crashed into the sidewalk. Cries of shock and concern came from people walking nearby.

Kody stood up and dusted himself off. "No worries, I'm okay!" He said reassuring the bystanders. "Alright, I'm on the ground." He picked up the hoverboard and inspected it for damage. After a sigh of relief, he threw it out in front of him and jumped on, speeding away toward the docks.

Gene's instructions took him unerringly toward Steel Harbor, Dock 22. Dodging streetwalkers and hooking onto the backs of cars going his direction, Kody moved quickly and efficiently.

Arriving at the scene, Kody hopped off his board and kicked it up into his hands. He brought it over his shoulder, and a spark reached out, grabbing the board and ripping it out of his hands. The magnetized bandolier was strong enough to hold it in place through the fabric of the overcoat.

"There are a lot of people here!" he whispered loudly to Gene as he ducked behind one of several stacks of wooden pallets.

"I'm zeroing in on your location now via satellite," Gene informed him.

"Dude, that's so cool!" Kody looked up to the sky and waved. He knew that Gene was working hard to hack into a different satellite feed. He called it 'feed jumping.' Gene said it was easy to do, so his signal was always on the move, making it harder for the government to track him. He also used a 'dummy pulse' to throw off anyone on his trail. Kody felt Gene should find a nicer name for it. If it had a pulse, it probably had feelings, too.

"Hello, did you hear what I just said?" Gene asked.

"Uh, nope. I missed it. I was thinking about other things, sorry."

"Can you hear what they're saying from your location?" Gene repeated.

"Nothing right now," Kody replied. "Just a bunch of people standing around, pointing and yelling at each other. Definitely gangs, though. It looks like a five-way standoff." Kody's view was limited from behind the pallets. He found a fire escape that led to the roof of a warehouse, and decided to climb up to get a better view.

When he reached the top, he found a man wearing a gray military-style outfit with black boots, straps, and pouches. He looked settled in like he'd been there awhile, watching the action below.

"What took you so long?" the stranger asked without looking up.

"Who are you?" Kody asked, "And how did you know I was coming?"

"When five of the city's most notorious gangs decide to hold a summit, you should expect me to be here."

Kody walked to the ledge and stood next to him. He didn't realize how much bigger the man in gray was; easily a head taller, with a thick, muscular frame. He tried not to stare too much. Instead he puffed out his chest to try and make himself look the part of a hero.

"Don't do that," Gray warned. "You'll put too much stress on your lungs. Just be natural."

Kody exhaled and slouched.

"Don't try to be something you're not; make the most of what you have."

"What?"

Gray looked down at him. "If you have a saw, you can't pretend it's an axe and use it to chop down a tree. Use what you have. You can get the same result; you just have to do it differently." Gray put his foot up on the ledge and leaned an elbow on his knee. "They've been out there now for about an hour, long before the cop showed up." He motioned towards Dock 22.

Kody looked over at the police officer. "He's in plain sight. Is he crazy?"

"Plain sight to us," Gray replied. "But on the ground, he's fairly well-hidden. Good thing, too. He's by himself and probably won't get any backup. The cops will handle small gang activity, but they won't go near something like this. This is too big for them. The gangs are gathering for something. Maybe a summit, I'm not sure. But something big is about to go down."

Gene's voice came through Kody's earpiece. "*Dispatch has ordered him to stand down and leave the area.*"

Kody didn't understand. "So, why is he still here?"

"He doesn't know any better," Gray replied. "Probably a rookie cop trying to make a name for himself; trying to be a hero. People often do things with the best intentions in mind, but don't stop to think of the consequences." Gray looked down at Kody.

"Was that directed at me? These guys can't hurt me," said Kody. "I'm bulletproof." He pounded a fist on his chest. "I have built-in armor."

"That's great kid," Gray said sarcastically. Then, in a more serious tone he added, "Can you breathe underwater?" He pointed out past the docks into the harbor. "The minute they find out you can't be hurt, they'll swarm you and drag you under. Unless you have super-strength, or something else you'd like to reveal to me?"

"Um, no, but I can fight." Kody clenched his fists.

"I've seen five-year-old children throw temper tantrums that will inflict more damage than you," Gray scoffed. "You're undisciplined. You think repelling a few bullets will save you from a mob of people?"

Kody's face went white under his mask. "You've been...watching me?" he asked. "How is that possible? You don't even know who I am under this mask."

"Please, *Kody*, don't underestimate me," Gray replied. "I'm very perceptive, and you'd be wise to listen and follow my lead. I'm here to help, and I can't risk you getting yourself killed."

The guy knew his name! Chills went up Kody's spine, as he tried to think if there was anyone else in his life who might know his secret. Mailman? Paperboy? A teacher? He couldn't think of anyone at all. Where had this guy been hiding?

"Can you turn invisible?"

"What does that have to do with anything?" Gray asked, as he continued watching the action down below.

"I don't know honestly. I almost never ask questions, but I've got to know—how do you know me?"

"I told you, I'm very perceptive," Gray said, giving away nothing. "All will be revealed in due time," he added. "But for now, keep quiet."

Kody hated to admit it but...

"He's right, Kody," Gene interrupted Kody's thoughts. *"If he's been spying on you and knows who you are, even with the mask, we have to trust that he should take the lead here."* Then he laughed, *"You've gone from hero to sidekick in one night!"*

"Well, that's dumb," Kody responded. "Okay, so what do we do? You can't fight them all either. You'll do it differently, but you'll get the same results as me." Kody felt good turning Gray's own words back on him.

"Well played, little hero," Gray acceded. "That's why we

aren't going to do anything. They are waiting for something. Whatever it is, we need to know about it." Then Gray motioned over to the cop, who was inching closer to the fray. "The only heroics you'll be doing tonight is saving that man's life. If he's spotted, you'll need to get him out of here. They'll try to goad you into fighting with them so they can outnumber you. Don't take the bait. Your priority will be to grab him, run, and if someone gets in your way, run through them. Don't stop for any reason."

Gene added some advice of his own, *"I am unsure of who this man is, but it sounds like he knows his stuff. Pay attention and follow his lead."*

Kody nodded.

He didn't like where this was going; he was his own hero. What if this guy dressed in gray was just trying to manipulate him for his own purposes?

Gray tapped him on the shoulder and pointed to a set of headlights emerging from the fog coming off the harbor. A black SUV rolled up, stretched out to the length of a limousine. The gangs parted as though there were some invisible forcing pushing them out of the way. Whoever was in that vehicle seemed pretty important.

Once the SUV stopped, three abnormally large men emerged and walked around to the driver's side door at the back of the limo.

Two of the men stood guard, their arms crossed, silently daring any gang member to step near them as the third opened the door.

A woman wearing a long, white coat stepped out. She wore a large brimmed hat that obscured her face from Kody's rooftop vantage point. Kody imagined it cast a shadow over her face so that nobody down there could see her either.

Gray motioned back towards the police officer, who was still inching closer to the scene. Any closer and he was sure to be discovered, which would break this whole gathering up before they could find out why everyone was here. Kody hoped the officer would hear his thoughts and stop moving. He heard the woman begin talking and his attention shifted back to her.

He couldn't make out what she was saying and she made no gestures, keeping her hands in her coat pockets. Whatever she had to say didn't take long. When she was done talking, she got back in the limo, which backed up about twenty yards, it's headlights still on. The three large men remained behind and pulled out sections of rope which they laid out between them, then stood at each point of the triangle they had made. The gangs began talking amongst themselves.

"What are they doing?" Kody asked.

"Shhh!" Gray hissed at him. After a few moments each gang sent one person from their ranks into the triangle. "They're looking for a champion," he whispered. "That woman is orchestrating all of this. She's recruiting only the best to help her."

"Help her with what?" Kody wondered aloud.

"Not sure. We'll have to see how it plays out." Gray settled in and prepared to watch.

"We can't just sit here and let it happen, can we?" Kody couldn't understand why Gray would be so relaxed about it. "It can't be good. This is organized crime. Whatever she's planning, it needs to be stopped."

Gray spoke calmly and showed no interest in looking away from the scene down below. "You couldn't stop them before, what makes you think you can stop them now, with three tanks down there? And who knows what else is inside that limo? If they don't do this here, they'll just do it somewhere else. Why not let them, so we can observe and learn?"

Kody clenched his fists and let out a low growl.

Kody settled in and watched, as much as it pained him to do so. From the five gangs, four men and one woman were now standing outside of the triangle. He couldn't believe that one of the gangs would send a woman to represent them. After a few tense moments of the gang bangers staring each other down, the woman stepped into the triangle and stared down the others. The four men began pushing each other toward the triangular ring as though none of them wanted to step in and fight her.

Kody was impressed they at least had the respect to not hit a woman. It was good to see criminals with some moral value.

He retracted that thought when a man wearing a white

tank top, black jeans, and a backwards baseball cap stepped in. The woman squared off, raised her fists in a guard, and stood motionless. The man held his fists up in a mockery of her stance. This evinced laughter and taunts from most of the other gang members, except for the ones who elected the woman to fight for them.

Bouncing up and down like a prize fighter, the man got worked himself up for the fight, prancing around the perimeter of the triangle. The woman kept her guard up, and allowed him to skip around the triangle like a fool. When he stopped in front of her, he rotated his shoulders a few times.

Without warning he threw a punch aimed at her head.

She sidestepped the blow, caught his wrist, and twisted it, forcing him to drop to a knee. She sent a palm strike into the back of his elbow, snapping his arm like a twig. She flicked off his hat dismissively and grabbed him by the bushy hair on his head, then slammed her knee into his nose. She let go and he fell to the ground, bloodied, beaten, and motionless.

Kody couldn't tell if he was dead or merely unconscious. He had underestimated her.

Another man entered the triangle, cracking his knuckles before dropping to the pavement to do a series of pushups. When he was done, he stood up and extended his hand to the woman.

She slapped it away. She was all business, and whatever it was the woman in white promised the winner, she was determined to have it. The man held out his hands in a defensive position, then looked over his shoulder and said something to the other two waiting for their turn.

Then, fast as lightning, he spun around and sent a back kick to her head!

She ducked under it like she knew it was coming. When his foot came down, he nodded in approval and began clapping his hands, condescendingly.

"Is it wrong that I'm starting to root for her?" Kody

whispered to himself. She was strong-willed, fast, and obviously being disrespected.

The man launched into her with a flurry of punches, which she blocked and parried with ease. She backed up as he continued to pressure her, but stopped dead in her tracks when her foot stepped on the rope. The man sent another spinning back kick into her midsection, and she caught him by the boot. Holding onto his leg, she stared the man down.

She ducked, then swept his other leg out from under him. He fell hard. When she came up, she dropped her foot onto his chest, causing the man to scream in pain. He grabbed at his chest with both hands, and she stepped over him as though he were beneath her notice.

She moved back to the middle of the triangle and waited for someone else to step in. The two remaining men talked for a moment, then both entered the triangle. Kody rose up from his crouch, but before he could say or do anything, Gray grabbed him by the shoulder with surprising strength and pulled him back down.

Kody watched as the two men approached her. She stood her ground and showed no fear. The one on her right, his flannel shirt opened to show his tattoos, feinted as though he were going to lunge. When she moved to block, the man on her left, sporting thick dreadlocks, punched her in the ribs. She let out a cry as she dropped to one knee. The first man tried to put his knee in her face, but she blocked it with her forearms and drove her fist into his groin. He went down—but so did she.

Kody looked away as the other gang member began to beat on her repeatedly. He heard her scream with each hit, but it wasn't long before her yelps were drowned out by cheers. He put his back to the ledge of the roof. Gritting his teeth, he punched the ground.

Seeing a woman beaten angered Kody so much, he didn't even notice when the cheering died down until he felt Gray's hand tugging on him to turn back around. "Leave me alone!" Kody hissed angrily. "I can't believe we just sat here and watched that. We shouldn't have let that happen!"

"Why?" Gray asked. "Because she's a woman? She chose to put herself in that position. If she's going to fight a bunch of men, her sex isn't going to act as a shield." Gray pointed toward the street. "Now, sit up and pay attention," he said. "Something else is happening."

Kody turned his gaze where Gray indicated. A quick glance at the cop revealed he was checking his firearm. *Good,* Kody thought. *Shoot both of those guys, they deserve it.* Movement elsewhere caught his eye, distracting his attention from the police officer.

A shadowy figure appeared from nowhere and approached the makeshift triangular ring. "Which gang did he come from?" Kody asked. "I didn't see."

"None of them. He just...showed up." Gray sounded concerned, which, in turn, concerned Kody.

Kody watched closely as the stranger stood in before the triangle fighting ring. His clothes were dark red, with bandages wrapped tightly around his outfit. The dock lights left much to the imagination, but for a brief moment Kody thought he saw what appeared to be some kind of mask.

"Is he-?"

"Yes," Gray cut him off. "He's wearing bandages over his face. They're not fresh, though. They're definitely stained."

"I know him!" Kody exclaimed. "He attacked me and my grand-" He caught himself before revealing too much. "He and some goons attacked me earlier."

The bandaged stranger pointed both hands at the two gang members who had just beaten down the defiant woman. Kody couldn't see if he had brought his pajama pals.

Two of the three giant men stepped away from their posts. They stood between the stranger and the fighters with their arms folded across their chests, determined not to let anyone disrupt their little contest. They looked down at the little man and smiled, their teeth large, crooked slates of enamel. They were bald, yet hairy everywhere else, including the bushy beards covering their thick necks.

They could have been clones of each other.

"Are you two brutes going to move, or will I have to go over you?" the stranger in red said flatly.

"Little man can't go over Quake."

"Rumble crush little man if he try."

"Oh really?"

The two gang members began to grow impatient, unsure if they should be fighting each other or waiting for Quake and Rumble to handle this outsider.

Movement on the ground caught Kody's eye. He watched as the female fighter regained consciousness and tried to pull herself up to her feet. "Yes," Kody cheered under his breath. "Get up."

Gray grabbed Kody's shoulder as he was leaned over into the action; any further and Kody would've fallen over the edge.

"Hey, *stugotz*," Tattoos shouted in a thick Italian accent. "What gang you from? You ain't have a chance to score juice from the Khan if you ain't part of no gang."

"You gon' done end up like dis little flowah if ya try mon." Dreadlocks kicked the struggling girl back down.

Kody clenched his teeth in anger. "Cowards."

In an eyeblink, the stranger jumped in the air. Placing a hand on the heads of Quake and Rumble, he propelled himself into a backflip, landing behind Tattoos and Dreadlocks. The twin brutes seemed confused as they looked around, wondering what just happened.

The red, bandaged stranger spun around like a dervish, sending a kick across the faces of both gang members. Kody pumped his fist with subtle joy. He didn't expect himself to take sides in all of this, but it felt good to watch a couple of bad guys, who had just ruthlessly beat up a woman, get put in their place. Whatever was about to happen to them, Kody was sure they deserved every bit of it.

Tattoo and Dreadlock looked stunned as they both

staggered backward. They had no time to recover as the red stranger began lunging fists into their bodies with a fury. He attacked both of them, simultaneously and repeatedly. They had no defense; all they could do was react as they flailed in pathetic attempts to defend themselves.

It became their job to absorb as many blows as possible and they performed as punching bags admirably. Kody got the distinct impression it could have been over even more quickly, and wondered if the stranger was pulling his punches to toy with them.

The man in red made several quick movements with his hands, then brought them back to his chest with a flourish. A glint of light caught Kody's eye as he did so, before he spun around into a crouch, one hand on the pavement in front of him, the other arm stretched out behind.

Kody shook his head in disbelief. Could all that have really happened so quickly?

The two fighters collapsed against each other, then fell into a heap on the ground. Something glistened in the dim light, slowly expanding from beneath the crumpled fighters and seeping across the pavement.

Blood.

With every blow, the stranger had stabbed each man, creating a bloodbath on the street. Knives had been used to tear into their flesh with each of those quick, precise strikes. A shiver traveled down Kody's spine, and he looked away.

Gray grabbed at Kody again, "Keep watching," he whispered.

Quake and Rumble had finally turned around, so that all three giants were facing Bloodbath (as Kody had mentally christened the red clad stranger), blocking him from Kody's view. In unison, all three of them reached out their hands as they slowly bore down on him.

Bloodbath did not move. He was waiting.

Kody could tell he wanted them to get closer, as close as possible, before he would make his move. Kody's body tensed up as though he were watching a movie back at his apartment. He could feel his palms getting sweaty inside his fingerless gloves. Could this little, violent, merciless man take down all three giants?

BANG! BANG! BANG!

Three gunshots shattered the tension and pierced the silence. Kody looked over at the lone officer of Port Haven's finest, who was foolishly standing out in the open, his badge held out for all to see, his gun high in the air.

"P.H.P.D.!" he yelled, as if anyone cared. He was young, but bold. He was not about to let anyone else get hurt. "Everyone, stand down! I'm only taking that man into custody." He pointed at Bloodbath. "The rest of you are free to go, provided there isn't any trouble."

A hush fell over the harbor, save for the muffled sounds of the ringing of a buoy and the lapping of water against the docks. Time stood still, trapping everyone in ice, motionless.

Kody breathed a sigh of relief. Maybe, he thought, this police officer had diffused the situation. Maybe everyone would just disperse, and he and Gray would be free to pursue the woman in white who started all this.

And then...

...all hell broke loose.

STEPHEN J MITCHELL

Kody watched as the five gangs began a rumble like he had never seen before in his life. He had, on occasion, seen a few kids fighting each other in the halls of his school. And, of course, he thought about his fight with Brett, Jared, and Paulie. This was different, though.

They had all assembled for a pit fight to choose a champion—a champion who would be awarded 'juice' from the Khan. They had boldly decided to hold this contest on the docks, where one police officer, hoping to stop the madness, committed a single act of stupidity, setting off a gang war; all because he wanted to bring one murderer into custody.

None of the original combatants were left standing after

Bloodbath came out of nowhere, fast as lightning and just as violent. He didn't belong to any of the gangs, and he moved seamlessly through the fray. Everyone else scrambled to punch, kick, stab, or club the nearest rival gang member, as Bloodbath dropped anyone within arm's reach, with deadly efficiency.

No one could lay a hand on him.

The officer was the only one not moving, stricken with fear at the scene before him. Bloodbath was carving a path through the chaos, straight toward him, and all Kody could do was stand and watch. He had already made several attempts to jump in, and each time Gray stopped him. Now, with an all-out war down there, Kody was certain there was no chance he would be allowed to get involved.

Gray growled. "Get down there and save the cop. I'll handle Marcus."

"Who's Marcus?" Kody took a deep breath and grabbed the ledge of the roof, trying to locate who Marcus might be.

"The insane person with the knives, butchering people."

"Oh, I've already named him Bloodbath. You need to be quicker." Hopping up on the ledge he added, "And for the record, 'Marcus' is not a very good villain name."

"It's not-" Gray interrupted himself. "Just get down there and save the cop!"

Kody shrugged his shoulders and jumped off the roof with a howl of excitement. "Wahoo!"

Gene yelled into his ear. *"You can't just keep throwing yourself from rooftops like that! You're bound to get someone killed!"*

"Well Genius..." Kody crashed into a stack of pallets. "You come up with something better, and I'll do it. Until then, it's reckless swan dives and crash landings!" He jumped up from the wreckage and ran towards the officer. A quick glance at the crowd to locate Bloodbath did him no good. There was too much chaos, too much fighting. He didn't have the advantage of being able to see everything all at once anymore.

He had to trust that Gray would take care of his end of

things.

"I have a few ideas in the works," Gene said. *"Do not concern yourself with Bloodbath. The guy you call Gray is already engaged with him."*

Kody loved the fact that Gene could see what he couldn't, although he was a bit confused how Gray made contact that quickly. "I just need a few moments to get this cop out of here, and then I can go help him."

"Don't move!" The cop turned his gun on Kody.

"Hey, relax," Kody said, holding his hands up to show his peaceful intent. "I'm one of the good guys. You need to get out of here!" Kody looked over his shoulder and saw that the fight was inching closer.

"I can't. My job is to serve and protect, and backup should be here any minute. I need to take that man into custody," the police officer pleaded.

Kody tried to reason with him. "Going back empty-handed is better than going back in a body bag. You need to go! NOW!" Something hit Kody in the back of the head.

Spinning around, he sent a backfist into the face of the man who had hit him. Looking back at the officer he pleaded one more time. "GO!"

The fight was on top of them now, so the officer holstered his weapon and began to engage. He took one man down quickly and slapped handcuffs on him. Someone else attempted to grab Kody by the neck with a frontal choke-hold.

Instinctively, Kody performed a *kubishimi* choke defense technique he had learned from Shihan Toshihiro. Using both hands, he snapped down on his attacker's elbows to break the hold. Then, with strength and precision, he jammed both fists into each side of his attacker's neck, pressing hard with his knuckles to restrict the blood flow to the man's brain. With a swift motion, he lunged forward and sent the man backwards to the ground.

As soon as he was free, another one came from behind him and put him in a bear hug. The officer was engaged with yet another gang member. There was nothing he could do to help him. Kody had to keep as many of these goons at bay as possible. Several other people started hitting him in the stomach and kicking at his legs. Staggering from the blows and the weight of the person on his back, he struggled to stay on his feet.

Kody flung himself backwards, carrying his attacker, and landed on his back. When he hit the ground, he felt something pop underneath him and the bear-hugger screamed in pain. Ignoring him, Kody rocked himself back and flipped up to his feet. In class, when he would practice that, Shihan told him that wasn't practical. Maybe he could teach his grandfather a thing or two!

A circle of gang members formed around him. Suddenly, he felt like a trapped animal. Someone from the circle dove at him and wrapped his arms around Kody's waist in an attempt to tackle him. But Kody spread his legs out to maintain his balance. He grabbed the back of the person's head, by his hair, then brought his knee up, smashed it into the man's nose, then shoved him aside.

Holding his fists up, Kody crouched and pivoted, knowing the next attack could come from any direction. They stood their ground, looking like a pack of lions that just found a zebra separated from its herd. Not wanting to keep his back to anyone for any length of time, Kody continued moving, his hands out to keep them at bay.

Then, one after another, they lunged, kicked, punched, and dove at him. He did his best not to be overwhelmed. He jumped over a diving man, dodged a punch from someone else, and countered with an uppercut. Catching a kick from another attacker, Kody grabbed the man's throat and stepped into him, placing his right foot behind his attacker's other leg and shoving him to the ground.

Since they couldn't hurt him, all he had to do was be patient and let them approach.

Kody decided if he fought with that kind of confidence, he should have no problem getting out of this. One by one, gang members came and each one of them was repelled. After another short melee, he looked around and saw six men lying on the ground in pain. The fighting on the harbor was thinning out, and the gangs were dispersing.

"I think we did it," Kody shouted as he looked around. "Where's Gray?"

"I don't know," Gene replied. *"I was paying attention to what you were doing."*

The officer shouted. "Look out!"

Kody tried to duck, not knowing what direction he was being warned to look out from, but it did no good. The force of the blow threw him from his feet, and he landed several feet away.

Kody looked up and saw Bloodbath looming over him, ready to fight. Bloodstained bandages covered his whole head except for his eyes and mouth. He held two small daggers, one in each hand, and had many more sharp weapons attached to his clothing.

"And who are you supposed to be," the stranger asked. "The sidekick?" He spoke with conviction, his voice scratchy and rough, as though he had swallowed a bag of razor blades.

Kody got up and gave himself a quick inspection. There were rips in his overcoat and shirt. Bloodbath had tried to stab him multiple times, and he didn't even see it happen! "I'm the person who's going to stop whatever all this is about." He waved his hands to indicate the entire harbor.

The stranger laughed in a way that sounded like it hurt. "You're a nobody who's in over your head," he replied. "Your friend and I have a...thing, and I'm not about to let his sidekick jump in and screw it all up!"

"I'm nobody's sidekick, Bloodbath."

"Don't call me that."

"Well I'm not going to call you Marcus, like Gray did."

"I have no name." Bloodbath pointed a knife to his own chest.

"Wait, did you say you have, 'a thing' with Gray? Like a

bro-mance?" Kody asked. "Look, I'm really not interested in what you two have. I want to know what this little gathering was all about." Kody began circling the stranger, hoping to make him feel trapped.

"It was about *this!*" He lunged at Kody, stabbing and slashing.

Kody swatted at the blows, but couldn't do anything about them. Bloodbath was just too fast. Frustrated, he decided to use his wit as a distraction.

"So, you're saying all this was about how bad you are at stabbing people?" His outfit was torn in several more places across the stomach and arms. "You're good at cutting cloth, though. Did you use to be a seamstress?"

Bloodbath looked at his blades, now bent and dulled from hitting Kody's impenetrable body. He threw them to the ground and drew two more. "You may be dagger-proof, but everything has a weakness" Attacking again, he easily struck his marks, tearing up more of Kody's clothing. His lunges were precise, and numerous, as he strove to find the chink in Kody's armor.

"Dagger-proof?" Kody mocked. "Try bulletproof! Those butter knives aren't going to even scratch me."

"It doesn't matter," he replied. "You're too slow to stop me from trying. You want to know the truth about what happened tonight?" He pointed with his blade. "Your answer is in the limo."

Kody looked at the limo and then back at Bloodbath. Gene cut in. *"Do not go over there, Kody. Come back to headquarters so we can go over tonight's events. Gray is gone, and the cops are almost on the scene!"*

Kody heard blaring off in the distance.

"Right." Ignoring everything Gene had just said, Kody ran towards the headlights of the limo, buried deep in the thick fog rolling in from the harbor. They beamed at him like the eyes of an angry beast. Bloodbath ran alongside him down the length of the pier. He easily pulled ahead of Kody and disappeared into the mist.

A chill ran down Kody's spine, but he kept going. It was getting harder to see, but he had to get to the woman in white. If she knew about the Khan, then he needed to ask her some questions.

Suddenly, he hit what seemed like a brick wall and he fell backwards.

"You no go dis way." It was the third giant. Much like the other two, Brick was tremendous in girth.

"If try, you die." His accent was thick, deep, and sounded like he spoke with a mouthful of molasses.

Kody heard a car door open and shut. Slamming his fist into the ground out of frustration, he picked himself up off the ground, and saw the giant shadowy figure standing over him. "Come on big fella, you can't hurt me," he said. "Did you see what just happened back there?" Kody was hoping Brick was as dumb as he was massive. "Now step aside before I confuse you with big words."

"What big words do you *know?"* Gene interjected.

"You fight like rabid animal," Brick said, "Rabid animals need put to sleep."

"Thanks, but no thanks," Kody replied. "I'm really not interested in taking a nap. All I want is what's inside that limo."

Quake and Rumble stepped up behind Kody. "Dis car not for you," Brick said. "Dis water, yes." The giant man pointed a thumb to the docks.

Kody realized this was exactly what Gray had warned him about. Was it possible he had been led into a trap? He should have never trusted Gray.

"Hello, little man," Brick snapped his fingers. "Is time to die now."

"Okay, don't say I didn't warn you!" Kody attempted to run around Brick, but a large hand grabbed his shoulder and forced him to the ground.

"Kody, I can't see you in the fog. what's happening?" Gene asked.

Kody fought to free his arm, only to be pushed down

harder. He dropped to one knee, and it was all he could do to prevent his arm from being bent in a way it wasn't designed to.

Another massive hand grabbed his other arm. Now on both knees, his arms outstretched, Kody was helpless. "Well Genius," he grunted as he struggled to free himself. "I think I'm about done here. I'd like to go home now!"

Back in Gene's cellar, the young savant frantically tried to find a security camera in the area that would give him a better angle as the fog thickened. After a moment he noticed something move in the background on his monitor.

"Hello little shadow, who might you be?" Gene mused to himself. He zoomed in on the image and let out a surprised yelp. *"What are you doing there?"*

"Getting my butt kicked at the moment!" Kody replied, thinking that Gene was talking to him.

At the harbor, Brick grabbed Kody by the throat and lifted him off the ground. Kody kicked and fought to get free, but nothing worked. "He squirm like little worm."

Kody tried to say something, but the pressure on his neck reduced any speech to little more than a gagging sound.

"Den use worm to catch fish!" Rumble said.

Kody continued to fight but his will began to fade, nothing he did could break him free of the brute's grip. With his air supply cut off, his vision began to fade. His fingers and toes grew numb and he lost track of what was happening. Lacking the strength to fight any longer, his limbs went limp and his world went black.

Darkness.

There was a sense of weightlessness coursing through Kody's body. He wasn't falling and he wasn't flying. He was just—there; floating in the darkness. There was no up or down, no left or right. Was he blind? Unconscious? Or maybe...

No! That couldn't be it. It couldn't!

He tried to scream, but nothing came out.

A small speck of light appeared. He reached for it, but it was much too far away. As it grew bigger, Kody couldn't tell if he was moving toward it, or if it was growing. It grew to the size of a penny; then a nickel, and then a quarter. Soon it was as big as a frisbee, and shortly after that it began consuming the darkness around it.

Kody tried to raise his hands to shield his eyes, but his limbs were dead. They felt heavy and tingly, as though they fallen asleep. The darkness was now dispelled and the light enveloped him completely.

"NOOOOO!" Kody screamed. The sound of his own voice scared him. He felt a gentle breeze on his face. It was warm and comforting, and he wanted to wrap himself up in that feeling. It made him feel safe. Spreading his arms out, he wanted to embrace the light and never leave this place. That was when he realized he could feel his arms and legs again. The tingling was gone, and as they moved, they left behind a blurry afterimage trail in their wake.

The breeze he felt grew stronger, and his hair began to whip around. A gray spec appeared in front of him, spinning like a vortex. As it got bigger, Kody knew this time he was falling. There was no weightlessness, just a heaviness pulling him fast into the vortex. He kicked his legs and flapped his arms, to no avail. It was useless to resist as he watched the warming light leave him. He didn't want it to go away. It had made him the happiest he'd ever been.

A loud thundering sound forced his attention back to the vortex.

Droplets began pelting his face, stinging with each hit. He tried to shield himself, but the drops flew through his arms as though they weren't there. A bolt of lightning streaked across the vortex, followed by another. A cape shot out of the gray and wrapped around him, covering him completely and protecting him from the stinging rain. He kicked and punched, trying to escape its grasp so he could see what was happening around him.

After some effort, he finally broke through, as the cape tightened up around his body, forming a layer of armor like a second skin. Creeping up his neck and over his face, it squeezed, suffocating him as it covered his head. He looked down at himself to his uniform, in black and gray instead of the black and green combination.

Suddenly, more flashes of lighting streaked past him, shredding his armor with each pass. Blood splattered from non-existent cuts and bubbled up, floating and swirling around him as the vortex picked up speed. As he descended towards the eye of the vortex, spinning out of control, he heard familiar voices whispering to him:

Forgive me, son.
Relax scamp, he just wants to meet you.
It's time to clear the air.
Hey, come back to us, will ya?
Someone did this to you.

The voices stopped with the lightning. There was no more wind, nor rain, nor vortex now. It was that eerie quiet found in the eye of the storm. Kody splashed deep into the water. The impact felt like getting swatted with a slab of concrete. He reached for the surface, trying to swim for the top but the more he tried, the deeper he sank. Wanting to end this merciless journey, he surrendered.

His body went limp.

A thin hand reached into the water after him. A familiar and gentle voice whispered, "Don't leave me."

"Kody!" He heard his name screamed out loud by a thousand banshee like voices. The darkness shattered and he opened his eyes.

"Callie?"

"Not even close." Gene's face slowly came into focus, changing from a blurry apparition to a recognizable figure. He pushed his glasses up on his face and held out a mug of water and a pill. "Here, take this," he said. "I surmise you will experience a massive headache now that you're awake. You have been unconscious for nearly two hours."

Kody looked around to discover he was back in Gene's basement. He was alive. His head hurt, and he wanted to take the medicine just to make it go away. He downed the pill, even though the sight of water made his stomach turn.

"What happened?" he asked.

"I am not entirely sure," Gene replied. "Although, I have been diligently working to put the pieces together. I lost visual and audio contact with you. At that point, I was left with no other option than to be there in person. I grabbed my taser and got to the harbor as fast as I could." Gene held his gadget up for Kody to see.

"You have a taser?" Kody shouted. He winced as his own voice caused him pain.

"Affirmative. I have a taser. Let us not get distracted by unimportant details." Gene set the device down and continued, "When I arrived at the harbor, you were the only one remaining."

"Where did I end up?" Kody asked, in a much quieter voice than before.

"I found you beneath the pier," Gene said. "Your costume, in spite of its water repelling construction, was soaked through. I have been unable to calculate exactly how long you were submerged. I estimate seven minutes. Your neck showed signs of strangulation, which would have simulated laryngospasm. That would explain why you did not drown immediately. Your air tube was restricted, preventing any water from entering your lungs."

Gene paced back and forth. He paused and thought for a moment before continuing. "The fact that your mask was pulled up over your nose would lead me to believe that the person who saved you performed CPR to keep you alive, then left before I arrived."

"Gray?" Kody asked, confused.

"Negative. I was surprised at the answer, myself," Gene answered. "At first I saw a shadow creeping around on the monitors. Then, with a different angle I captured her image on screen. She saved your life, Kody."

"She?" Kody felt embarrassed and flattered at the same time. He wondered if CPR counted as kissing. Now he just needed to know who the lucky girl was. "She who?"

"Callie Cruz."

"Callie!"

"Is that concern or enthusiasm?" Gene asked.

"Can it be both?" Kody couldn't believe what he was hearing. He did a quick 'breath check' hoping she wasn't grossed out when she put her mouth on his. It wasn't awful, so he shrugged and moved on to his next thought. "What was Callie doing out by the docks in the middle of a gang war?"

Gene went to the monitors and started tapping away at the keyboard. "While you were recovering, I reviewed the video feeds recorded while I was retrieving you. They showed her struggling to pull you out. Because I was not manning the cameras, there was no zoom or focus, only the natural camera angle to view. I checked the other security camera feeds for different angles, none of which were very clear, mind you, and it seems there is no other conclusion for me to arrive at than that—"

"I'm sorry," Kody interrupted. "I stopped paying attention after 'while you were recovering.' The whole CPR thing keeps running through my head, and the images are distracting me. Can you give me the short version of whatever it was you just said?"

Gene took a deep breath and exhaled slowly. "I don't know why she was there, but she was."

"Well, we need to figure it out."

Gene leaned back and stared at the monitors while stroking his chin. "It's too random," he mused. "Nobody just hangs around the docks, especially someone as young and attractive as Callie. With all of those gang members, she would have been an easy target for a violent crime. Unless..." Gene's voice trailed off and he rewound the video footage. Taking off his glasses he leaned in to inspect the video closer.

"Is your screen dirty? You can use my shirt if you want." Kody tugged at his damp and tattered shirt.

"Gross. I don't want that thing touching my screen." Gene held his hand out to keep Kody away. "There!" He pointed to a face that looked familiar to him. "Isn't that Callie's dad?"

Kody leaned in to see where Gene was pointing. "That's him all right," he confirmed. "Doesn't surprise me, really. I mean, the guy is an abusive alcoholic who shot me for being in his tree. Why not add gang member to the list?" He backed away and gripped at his hair in frustration. "Why didn't she tell us? We're her friends."

Gene turned in his chair. "Same reason you haven't told her you're bulletproof, I suppose," he replied. "You just don't know how someone is going to react, and she's probably afraid we'll look at her differently. As a Latina, can you get more stereotyped than having your dad be in a gang? Brett called her an illegal immigrant in front of the entire cafeteria. This probably confirms why she was so upset by it."

"She's my friend," Kody countered. "I wouldn't judge her because of her dad. I'm the last person on the planet who should do that."

"Maybe you should tell her your secret then," said Gene. "If you open up, it might make things easier for her. Then maybe you can get back to daydreaming about CPR."

"Har, har." Kody rolled his eyes as his cheeks flushed with embarrassment. "Speaking of getting back, how did you get me back to your basement?"

"I used your hoverboard to push you to the roadside, then called a ride service."

"How did you explain the mask and stuff?" Kody asked. "And, you know, not being old enough to order a ride service?"

"I used my parent's credit card and a fake ID I've relied on in the past. All I need to do is sound angry and offended that they're assuming I'm a child because of my height. Then I just mix in some big words because they tend to confuse people."

"Tell me about it," Kody replied. "Actually, don't. I'm already starting to zone out."

"Everyone worries about offending others these days," Gene said. "So, if all else fails, I just pull the race card. That trumps everything."

"You're losing me now. How did you explain the mask?"

"I told them you're a massive nerd who enjoys cosplaying and LARPing."

"Of *course* you did." Kody rolled his eyes. "Although, it's not really far from the truth, I guess."

"Precisely," Gene smiled.

"I need to call Callie."

Gene didn't question the sudden jump in the topic. As usual, he just tried to keep up. "I think you should just be grateful she was in the right place at the right time, and not push the issue right now."

"I don't really care what you think right now, Gene," Kody replied. "My head hurts, my body aches, and I wouldn't feel either of those if Callie hadn't saved me. She needs to know I'm grateful." He hung his head. "Some hero I turned out to be."

"Don't be so hard on yourself," Gene said. "You were outnumbered. I would say that, given the situation, you fared quite well." He hoped a compliment and a distraction would assist him in re-focusing his friend's thoughts. "Right now, we should concentrate on deciphering Gray's motives and finding the connection between Bloodbath and the woman in white."

Kody thought for a moment. His mind was a jumbled mess of things he couldn't sort through. "All I know is Gray said he would handle Bloodbath. And Bloodbath said that he and Gray had a 'thing'—whatever that's supposed to mean. Gray called him Marcus, Bloodbath said he doesn't have a name, and now my brain is confused."

"It clearly means they have had some history," said Gene. "We just don't know the 'how' and 'why' of it. I feel that it would be pertinent to put some pressure on Gray the next time you meet. We need answers."

Gene slid his chair over to a computer and began

tapping away. "The woman in the limousine, Bloodbath, Gray, five gangs and their champion fighters." Gene spoke the words as he typed them in, then rubbed at his chin.

"Don't forget the Khan," Kody reminded him. "Who apparently runs a terrorist organization that's out to get me."

"How is it you have managed to draw the ire of so many people?" Gene wondered aloud.

Kody shrugged. "Beats me. The most I can draw are stick figures, and I don't even know what an 'ire' is!" He threw his hands up in frustration.

"Good to have you back." Gene smiled and decided to let Kody's comment go without correction this time.

Kody spent the rest of the weekend resting. Television news reports delivered mixed accounts as to whether or not an alien had shown up downtown, or if there was a movie being filmed. Nobody was sure what to make of it.

When Callie called and asked if he heard about the person zipping around Port Haven on a magic skateboard, Kody just shrugged it off and said he had been too busy training with Shihan Toshihiro to notice.

Kids in school were buzzing about it too. 'The flying man' had become a pretty popular topic. Everyone wanted to know who he was and how he did what he did.

Kody wanted to go back out after school, but he had

that commitment to the 'Emerging Leaders' program. He had no intention of participating, though. Instead, he planned to sneak off to the International Bank of Port Haven, to investigate what his father had hidden there.

After school dismissed, a bus took the ELPH program students to one of the local homeless shelters. Gene and Kody slowly worked their way to the back of the line, so they could slip out unseen. It wasn't difficult to do; there were a lot of kids involved in the program, not to mention the great Brett Walker, whom Dean Winters loved so much. For the entire ride downtown, Brett kept giving him dirty looks.

Shihan Toshihiro had told Kody he should try to make peace with Brett by getting to know him better as a person, and, if all went well, possibly mend any bad feelings between them. Kody kept thinking about how Brett's hand was wrapped in a bandage that went all the way past his wrist. He didn't know if the hand was broken or sprained, and he couldn't be sure without asking.

He was pretty sure that wouldn't be an appropriate ice-breaker.

That was a conversation for another day, though. Kody had more important concerns pressing on him, as he played with the metal key in his pocket, turning it over and over in his hand.

Once everyone was inside the shelter, he and Gene broke off from the line formation and walked to the International Bank several blocks away.

He didn't go downtown very often. Even though he had just been there, cruising around on his hoverboard and then nearly getting drowned, he didn't respect how big the city truly was. Looking up, he noticed the buildings peaked high into the sky. He wondered if the taller one's ever ended; they extended up so high they seemed to disappear into the clouds. Being a coastal city, Port Haven always seemed to be covered in a fog that hid the tops of its skyscrapers.

Staring at them made Kody dizzy, like they were rocking

back and forth, until he realized that he was the one that was rocking.

A few raindrops began to fall, and Kody focused his eyes back on the sidewalk in front of him. He put his hoodie up and continued to follow Gene. To his knowledge, Gene never left his parents' wine cellar except to go to school, so how could he possibly know where the bank was located?

When they finally stopped, Kody looked up and saw the steps leading up to the bank. The staircase was so wide that, even on the busiest days, people could go up and down without bumping into each other. The gold letters 'IBoPH' were carved into the brownstone above the glass doors. There was a large potted tree on either side of the steps, a small reminder in a city full of steel that trees still existed.

When they entered the bank, Kody was amazed at the enormity of the interior. They each had to go through a checkpoint, monitored by an armed guard. Kody emptied his pockets into a tray: his wallet, keys, cell phone, some loose change, a paperclip, a piece of lint, and, of course, the metal key. All of that went through an x-ray machine, while he walked through a metal detector.

Once he was through, he was patted down by another guard wearing blue latex gloves. The whole time, Kody's attention was on the impossibly high ceiling. From the outside, the bank didn't seem this big. There was a second floor, but the middle of the bank was all open, allowing him to look straight up at the circular blue dome in the middle of the roof.

After the pat down was over, the guard handed him back his things.

Everything except the paperclip.

A middle-aged man in a dark suit and expensive-looking red necktie approached Gene and Kody with his hands clasped together. "Good afternoon boys. I'm Mr. Porter-Schmidtenhousen, at your service. Are you lost? Or perhaps you were just looking to get out of the rain?" He was tall. Several heads taller than Kody in fact, and slender with slicked back hair and a pencil thin mustache.

"No, Mr. Porter-Schmidten...uh...housen?" Kody struggled to say the name in its entirety. "Can I call you Mr. Porter?"

"No."

"Mr. Po?"

"Never."

"Mr. P?"

"Ugh, perish the thought!" The man put the back of his hand dramatically to his forehead.

"Okay then." Kody rolled his eyes. "Actually, I'm here to get something that I think belongs to me." He looked at Gene and shrugged his shoulders.

"Really?" The man looked surprised. "Oh, I see," he smiled. "The lost and found is up by the guard station."

"I didn't lose anything," Kody said, slightly irritated. "You're holding something for me. A safe deposit box?"

The strange man gave him a confused look. During the awkward silence, Kody felt so nervous he began to sweat. It felt like the temperature shot up by 100 degrees. Unsure of himself he added, "I think?"

"Oh," the man's tone suddenly became depressed. "Come to collect your silver spoon, I suppose. Typical. Mommy and daddy die in a mysterious accident, and suddenly the children show up to inherit their fortune and take the money out of my bank." The man turned and began walking. "Follow me."

Kody and Gene looked at each other and then followed him. They went to an office where he motioned for them to close the door as he sat behind a desk. "Please, sit." He held his hands out to the two chairs in front of them. Once they were seated, he leaned forward and folded his hands on the desk. "Now, you say we're holding something for you?"

"Yes sir, Mister..." Kody looked at Gene who nodded back at him, "Porter-Schmidtenhousen?"

"Not bad. Now, what's your name?" Mr. Porter-Schmidtenhousen turned, hands poised over the keyboard on his computer, waiting for Kody's response.

"Ko-,"

"-orso!" Gene interrupted, "His name is James Corso."

The man raised an eyebrow, confused at the response. "Really? The smaller, less imposing, child speaks!"

"I'll have you know I'm not a child, and I'm offended that you assumed as much."

"Do forgive me sir, I meant no offense."

Gene smiled and looked at Kody who rolled his eyes.

"So," Mr. P. said. "James Corso, you say?"

Kody looked at Gene in confusion, but played along. "Yeah, that's me. James Corso. My friends call me Jimbo." Kody shot a frown at Gene. "His name is Dexter."

"That's right," Gene agreed.

"See, we know each other's names because we're friends," Kody smiled.

"Yes," Gene said. "I call him Dex and he calls me Jim."

"Dex." Kody corrected.

"We're friends." They both said in unison.

The man sat and thought for a moment, "Right," he replied, drawing the word out. "So why did you have to tell me his name?"

Gene replied, as calmly as he could. "He was not going to tell you the truth. He is quite the joker you see. We call him 'Joker' Jim because he frequently plays jokes on people. We all know that you need a security code and not his name, so he was just going to be funny and make up a fake name. Right, Joker Jim?"

"Uh, yeah...that's it! I can't resist a good practical joke." Kody laughed nervously. He finally realized that Gene was trying to protect his identity. If someone tracked them down and found out they were here, at least the different name would throw them off the scent.

Protect your identity.

That's rule number one of being a superhero, and seeing as how they were knee deep in superhero shenanigans, he needed to be careful about who knew his name.

The strange man broke out into laughter. Kody and Gene just looked at each other uneasily and laughed along with him.

"Oh, you boys gave me a good laugh today. Very good, very good. Now go ahead and give me that security code. If you have the security code, that's the important thing," he said. "Names are mere constructs of society meant to place labels on us. You honestly think I was born with my name?" The man wiped a tear from his eye and cleared his throat. "I chose it as a mockery of the system of which I will never conform to."

Kody looked at the man awkwardly and pulled the metal key out of his pocket and handed it to him.

Mr. P. entered the information into the computer, his eyes lighting up as the information displayed on the terminal. "Glory be! We've been holding this box for quite some time! Let me get that for you." He got up and left the room, leaving the door open behind him.

"That was a good call on the name thing." Kody whispered. "How did you know everyone just uses a security code here?" Kody looked over his shoulder, through the open door. He watched as people stood in a line at the counter, waiting to make their transactions.

"This is an international bank," Gene said. "While they engage in legal activities, they handle accounts from all over the world. People prefer anonymity because of how they acquired their wealth. The bank is here to make money by providing a safe haven for all types of people to do business, criminals and saints alike." Gene took off his glasses and proceeded to clean them with a cloth from his pocket.

Kody raised an eyebrow. "Isn't that immoral?"

Gene sighed. "Depends on your perspective," he replied. "Some believe morality is defined by what has been carved into a stone tablet six thousand years ago. Moral or not, international banks are a way for people to protect their assets, regardless of how they were acquired."

"What?" Kody said as he continued to be distracted by

the people in the lobby. "I'm sorry, I wasn't paying attention. I have no idea what you just said, but it sounded important, and I appreciate you." Kody said.

The longer someone talked, the harder it was to stay focused on what they were saying. Gene had a tendency to be extra wordy at times, so on occasion it was extra hard for Kody to pay attention. And even when Kody did, Gene used a lot of words he didn't understand. It was a small miracle they understood each other at all.

Gene placed his glasses on his nose and pushed them up on his face. "In short, it is immoral but necessary."

"That's dumb," Kody said. "They could bankrupt a drug lord and put him out of business, or close an account to cripple a terrorist like the Khan." Kody's eyes widened at the possibilities.

"They could also rip funds away from a cancer research foundation." Gene watched Kody's face droop after tasting reality. "Anonymity is the best way for an international bank to do business with everyone. There are too many conflicts of interest not to."

"So, they stay out of everyone's business so they can do business with everyone?"

"Precisely."

"How does the government allow that to happen?"

"You think politicians are any better?" Gene asked. "They label it 'diplomatic immunity' and look the other way. Power corrupts, Kody."

Kody grunted in disapproval. "If I ran a business, I'd only do business with good people. Money wouldn't be important to me. If you were a jerk or a bad person, I wouldn't want your money."

"Easy to say now," Gene argued. "But when every dollar matters to stay in business, those choices become harder."

"Whatever, I'm broke as a bad joke, and I will be until I croak. But I won't take blood money from anyone."

At that moment, Mr. P. returned carrying a small metal box. He closed the door behind himself and sat down at his desk, gently setting the box on the desk. He tapped at the top of it and entered something into his computer. Kody stared at the box and wondered what could be inside of it.

"Oh!" The man exclaimed.

Kody and Gene both jumped in their seats.

"I guess you should open it now?" Kody said.

"Well perhaps you'd like to. It *is* your box after all," Mr. P. handed the metal key back to Kody.

He could feel his palms getting sweaty with nervousness. This was it. Whatever was in this box was what his father wanted him to have. "Are you sure?"

"Please do," he said. "I need to take inventory of the contents to make sure everything is accounted for." Mr. P. leaned forward in his chair and folded his hands on the desk, his eyes wide with anticipation.

It made Kody feel very uncomfortable.

Kody set the key into a rectangular depression, like a puzzle piece, and looked to Gene for affirmation. A red light circled around the key, then turned green. The lock clicked, and the top popped up a little bit. He opened the lid and looked inside. There was a USB drive nestled in a foam casing.

Kody pulled it out and held it up. "That's it?"

Mr. P. typed a few things into his computer and waited a moment. When the screen flickered with new information he said, "One USB drive. Yes, that is all that is supposed to be in the box." He reached his hand out for it. "I can take a look to see what is on it, if you'd like?" The smile was creepy, but genuine. The man seemed to want to help.

Again, Kody looked at Gene, unsure if this was a good idea. Again, Gene nodded. He handed the drive over and quickly rubbed his sweaty palms on his jeans. Mr. P. started tapping away at his keyboard and moved the mouse around, clicking here and there.

He inserted the drive and waited. "You know, as an international bank we hold all kinds of things in safe deposit boxes. We don't just store people's money. Wouldn't it be funny if this was just a blank drive?"

"Ha, yeah, real funny," Kody said, thinking it wouldn't be funny at all, considering his father's death, his mother's disappearance, and him being targeted by the Khan were all related to this little memory stick.

"Well, now." Mr. P. turned the computer screen so Kody could see it for himself. "As I suspected. You've just become a very rich boy."

Kody's jaw dropped as he looked at the screen. There were a bunch of numbers filling a grid. There were a lot of commas and decimal points, numbers upon numbers. He couldn't make sense of it all, as the numbers seemed to dance around on the screen.

He blinked several times to make the dancing stop. "What am I looking at?" he asked.

"This here," Mr. P. pointed to the top left part of the screen, "is the initial deposit." He moved his finger down the screen. "This is all the interest the account has gained every month over the years." Then he brought his finger down to the lower right-hand side of the screen to another number

"This is your current balance," he said dramatically.

Kody looked at the number, then rubbed his eyes and looked at the number again.

It was over *fifteen million dollars*!

Now he understood the danger he was in. His father had stolen money from the people who had funded his research. Research that had turned him into an indestructible human being. Those people had probably came looking for their money, the research or even both.

His father must have realized if they were allowed to build an army of bulletproof soldiers, the world would be run by terror and chaos. Rather than turn everything over to the Khan, his father split everything up, and now Kody had it all. He had to figure out how to hide the money so nobody could know about it.

He looked at Gene, who was staring at the computer

monitor in awe. It was a moment before Kody was able to speak.

"Mr. Porter-Schmidtenhousen?"

"Yes?"

He swallowed hard to remove the lump in his throat. "I'd like to open an account, please."

The following day, Kody was called down to speak with Dean Winters. Did someone notice he skipped out on Emerging Leaders, he wondered? It was probably Brett. The way Brett looked at him, he must have known something was up. He probably watched him and Gene sneak out. Kody cursed himself for being so careless. He didn't know why he agreed to try and reach out to that jerk, as if he could ever be friends with someone like Brett. This visit meant he got ratted out and was no doubt on his way to another week of detention.

Or worse, suspension!

Kody slouched in his seat, not looking forward to confronting Dean Winters again. He was pretty sure the dean hated him. How else could he explain the man's constant defense of a bully? So what if Brett was good at sports? That didn't give him the right to be a constant jerk to everyone.

The seconds on the clock ticked away slowly. The hallways were empty, as every student, minus a few stragglers, had all gotten to their classes by now. His leg started bouncing restlessly, and he squirmed in his seat. What was taking so long? He hated sitting still. Maybe this was part of his punishment. Winters must know he had to keep moving or he'd go crazy. Kody's only conclusion was that Winters planned to torture him. His head flopped back in frustration, and he stared at the ceiling. He never noticed the holes in the tiles before. He wondered how many there were.

His phone buzzed.

Pulling it out of his pocket, he flipped it open and saw a text from Callie. She wanted to wish him luck—even sent a 'thumbs up' emoji. She was in study hall, which means she was actually in the 'bullpen' working on the school newspaper. She never needed study hall to get her work done, so she repurposed that time. *The Bannerville Bulletin* carried random nonsense from students who wanted to write. Kody skipped over them. Except for Callie's articles. He read all of those, because, even if it was about Chess Club, it felt important to him. Which was weird, because he didn't like chess. The game had too much sitting still and doing nothing.

A student ran past the Dean's office.

Kody looked over his shoulder, then at the clock. Class had started ten minutes ago. He smiled, because he'd be running too if he was that late. And the whole way there, he'd be trying to come up with an excuse about where he was. Not that the teachers ever bought that his bladder was as weak as he claimed. He laughed at how silly it sounded, but no matter how creative he tried to be, 'I had to pee' was his default excuse.

He pulled his phone out to look at Callie's text again. Something about it made him feel better about sitting there with nothing to do.

Suddenly, he heard some yelling out in the hall. Whatever it was, it had to be more interesting than this boring old room. He went to the door and opened it to see what was going on.

Miss Jansen, from the main office, came sharply over the PA system just as he opened the door. "Attention! This is an active shooter alert. We ask that all students and staff members shelter in place. This is *not* a drill. Shelter in place."

Active shooter? At Bannerville High? Kody couldn't believe what he was hearing, especially from Miss Jansen, whose voice was always so calming, like Callie's was.

Callie!

Kody ran out into the hallway where it was eerily quiet. Fire drills had the constant ringing of bells that was loud and distracting. Kody decided this silence was worse. It was scary. He heard a muffled pop. The shooter was downstairs! He needed to get to the bullpen on the first floor. He needed to make sure Callie was safe!

He swore under his breath and ran down the stairwell, skipping several steps at a time. His foot slipped on a step, and he careened down and into the wall of the stairwell. He quickly got up, unharmed, and finished his descent down the next flight of stairs.

If it was a shooter, he hoped he ran into him. Kody knew he'd be safe and also be a hero in the process! He smiled, wanting to see the expression on the shooter's face when the bullets just bounced right off him!

When he got to the bullpen he entered slowly.

"Callie?" he whispered.

"Kody, hide!" Callie poked her head up and waved for him to come over to her.

"Kody!" A man's voice came from behind him. He ducked and spun around, but it was only Dean Winters. "Get in the classroom and stay there until we clear the area."

"What? No, I can help," He protested.

"Get in there, now!" Dean Winters grabbed him by the arm to push him into the room.

"Kody!" A voice in the hallway.

Dean Winters let go of Kody and both of them turned toward he voice.

Brett Walker stood ten feet away, holding a gun out in front of him with both hands. The wrap he wore just a day before was gone. His hand was swollen and bruised. "You're looking at your handiwork, aren't you?" He raised his arm in the air. "Don't worry about that. Playing sports gets me access to some of the best painkillers. It feels just fine." He waved it around, keeping the gun aimed at Kody.

Dean Winters raised a hand. "Just relax son," he said. "Whatever's bothering you, we can work through this. There's no reason needs to get hurt."

Brett Walker turned the gun on Dean Winters. "Yes. There is."

"Kody, get back into the classroom," the Dean pleaded under his breath.

"No!" Brett spat. "He's the one I want. He ruined me. All the pressure of having to get good grades. Playing my hardest only to get criticized that it's still not good enough. Now my hand is broken because of you! You think any college wants to recruit a quarterback with a broken throwing hand?"

"Dude, you punched me in the face!" Kody argued.

"Kody, don't!" Dean Winters said, putting his arm out in front of him. "Brett, listen to me. It's not the end of the world. We'll work through this. We'll get you the support you need."

"Yeah?" Brett turned the gun on him. "You don't know anything about what kind of support I need. You sit in your office without a care in the world. Meanwhile, I'm mocked if I have a bad game. Get ridiculed by my dad if my grades are bad. I have to do things I don't want to do, just to stay in the game. Now I'm hooked on these friggin' painkillers.

And you know what? I like it! I don't want to feel anything anymore!"

"Brett," Kody said. "I didn't know, dude."

"Nobody knows!" Brett shouted. "But you know what they do know? They know that I got beat up by you. A low-life, charity case, dirtbag who just wants to drag everyone else down with him!" Brett pointed the gun angrily at Kody.

Kody closed his eyes. If that's what Brett thought about him, there would be nothing he could do to convince him otherwise. Not now anyways. He should have reached out to him sooner. Why did he put it off?

Kody took a deep breath. "Brett, I didn't mean to hurt you. I had no clue what you were dealing with. You and I, we aren't so different. Hand over the gun and we can talk. Maybe even be friends."

"No! I can't be seen with you and your freaks," he said. "I'll be the laughing stock of the school. I'd never hear the end of it. Here, or at home"

"Freaks? My friends are good people. We don't go around harassing kids that are different. You harass me all the time," Kody said. "We all have problems, but you don't see me walking in here waving a gun around. Put it down and let's talk!"

"Brett," Dean Winters pleaded. "Put the gun down, now, before anyone gets hurt. You won't be in trouble. I promise."

"What?" Kody stared at the Dean who stood next to him. He couldn't believe his ears. He wouldn't even get in trouble for this? Kody decided it was time to remind Brett of all the things he should be grateful for. "Your parents have money, dude. You're smart, and you're a super-talented athlete. Don't throw it all away because I'm a screw-up who doesn't understand what you're dealing with."

"Shut! *Up!*" Brett screamed. He looked down the sight of his gun and pulled back on the slide, putting a bullet into the chamber of the gun. A bead of sweat trickled down his forehead. His hands were shaking as the gun trembled in his grip.

His finger squeezed the trigger.

POP!

Kody closed his eyes and flinched, even though he knew he could absorb the hit without getting hurt. It was a reflex. Getting shot at was still a little scary. But he felt nothing— not even a thumping against his chest. Was his invulnerability still developing, he wondered. Was this what it was going to be like?

Then he heard Callie scream. Opening his eyes, Kody saw Dean Winters laying on the floor, blood pooling out from beneath him. Brett was nowhere to be seen.

"Kody!" Callie ran to him and put her arms around him.

"Callie, I need you to stay here with Winters," Kody said.

"Where are you going?"

"I need to stop Brett before he hurts anyone else."

"Kody, no!" she pleaded. "He'll shoot you, too!"

Kody peeled her off of him. She was shaking. How could he protect her and go after Brett? "I can't let someone else get hurt because of me," he told her. "I need to stop him."

"Kody!"

"Call for help!" he shouted back at her as he rushed down the hallway.

Kody ran as though his life depended on it. Not his, of course, but definitely someone else's. While Brett clearly intended on killing him, now that he had shot Winters, who knows what he might try doing, or who he might try hurting?

He followed the sound of Brett's footsteps echoing through the silent hallways. The school had never felt so empty, even though Kody knew it was full. He saw Brett up ahead, down the long hallway leading to the sports complex and the football field.

Brett turned and fired a few errant shots. One hit a locker. One whizzed by Kody's head. The third hit Kody in the shoulder, spinning him around but not enough to stop him. Brett ran out of the building, and Kody continued to chase him out onto the football field. They were alone there. Brett was standing on the school's logo at midfield. He was pointing the gun at Kody.

"I hate you," he seethed.

"Brett, whatever happened we can work this out," Kody said. "I know things have been crazy, but you have to put the gun down so no one else gets hurt. Please."

Brett pulled the trigger and a bullet hit Kody square in the chest. Kody looked down at his ripped shirt and brushed it off.

"Go ahead, Brett. If that's what you need to do, pull the trigger again. Get it out of your system." He took a step forward.

"What the—?" Brett looked at Kody in fear. "What *are* you?" He fired off two more shots. One missed Kody, the other hit him in the stomach.

Kody continued to advance, unharmed.

"Leave me alone!" Brett wailed. Then he put the gun to his own head. "Back off or I'm pulling the trigger!"

"Brett, I don't know what to say," Kody said calmly. "I honestly wish I did. You've got things going on and my attitude didn't help that. I just thought you were a big jerk. I have trouble understanding these things because my brain doesn't work the way it's supposed to. But I realize now that I should have taken the time to try and be your friend. To listen. Let's start over." Kody paused and then added, "I'm here for you and you don't have to feel alone anymore."

Brett's hand trembled. His eyes were watery and red. "You know what?" he said "Even if you did, I probably wouldn't have listened."

Brett pulled the trigger but nothing happened. He pulled it again. And again. Kody breathed a sigh of relief, realizing the magazine was empty. He walked up to Brett, who had dropped to his knees and was staring at the gun.

"No, no, no, no. I shot you!"

"No, you didn't." Kody lied.

"You should be dead. I had enough bullets. I shot you,

you're dead. That's real life. You aren't bulletproof. Real people aren't bulletproof!"

When the cops arrived at the field, they found the two boys on the football field. Brett kept going on about how he had shot Kody several times, and how Kody hadn't been hurt. After inspecting Kody's clothes, one police officer questioned him about the holes.

"All my clothes are like this," Kody answered. "I fall off my skateboard, I train at 'Tatakai Aikido', and I'm also a bit of a klutz. And since most of my clothes come from the thrift store, they just don't last very long to begin with."

The officer seemed to be okay with the explanation, as Kody's heart pounded in his chest with fear and adrenaline.

They handcuffed Brett and confiscated his weapon. Brett yelled in protest but the cops just ignored him. Not wanting to upset the teen who had just gone through a psychotic episode, they simply nodded and agreed. They asked him to tell them more about what happened, while at the same time reminding him that he had the right to remain silent.

Brett had no desire to be quiet. As he was led off to the squad car, he yelled back at Kody. "You're not bulletproof! I'll find a way to stop you! This isn't over! You're *nothing*! I'm the hero of Bannerville High. They love *me*, not *you*!"

When classes resumed, everyone had something to say about what had happened.

"What happened to Brett?"

"Thank goodness for lockdown drills."

"Why are we even in school today?"

"We need more gun control."

"He clearly had mental problems."

The voices in the auditorium rang loud and clear. There was worry. There was pain. There were jokes. And there was silence, which, eerily enough, Kody felt was the loudest. Everyone looked at him with judgement. They each had a version of the story to tell and, for the most part, they were all wrong.

How Brett was apprehended was an evolving story that spread like wildfire. Some say he turned himself in, others say he was taken down as he tried to escape.

"I'm so happy you're okay," Callie said as she sat to Kody's left. The auditorium was buzzing as all the students were called in for an assembly to discuss the events that occurred.

The school had been closed for several days, as counselors were made available. Life must go on, however, and while a lot of students may have enjoyed the time off, others needed to get back so things could start to feel normal again.

Nothing would ever truly be normal though. Bannerville High School would now be just another school in the news—another statistical data point for people to argue about, as politicians and citizens promoted opposing viewpoints about the best course of action. Meanwhile, the students who were affected just tried to sort it all out, wondering if it would happen again while the echoes of gunshots continued to reverberate through their memories.

"So, Brett's intention was to kill...*you*?" Gene asked in a puzzled voice. "It's confusing to me, because one would think it would be the other way around."

"Gene!" Kody and Callie said in unison.

"I'm just saying that typically the bullied outcast is the stereotype for these things."

Kody said nothing.

Callie tried to offer some perspective. "Well, he was clearly dealing with issues nobody else knew about. I wish someone would have reached out to him sooner." She put her hand on Kody's forearm and gave it a gentle squeeze. Callie knew her friend intended on trying to make peace with Brett, but for whatever reason he never did.

Kody's silence made it clear he felt responsible.

As Principal Clark took the stage, the buzz in the auditorium quieted until you could hear a pin drop. One person coughed, and it resounded throughout the room.

The counselors who were invited to the school were standing behind the Principal, ready to answer any questions. The most noticeable guests were the ones standing off to the sides, though.

Police officers.

Principal Clark spoke for roughly twenty minutes without a single question asked. Not one word was uttered from the student body. When the assembly ended, everyone in attendance made their way out into the halls, where all that was heard was the shuffling of feet and the murmur of a few voices.

And then, in almost no time at all, the hallways were as noisy as they ever were.

Everyone had left the auditorium except Kody, Callie, and Gene.

"It should have been me," Kody said in a tone barely audible.

"Kody, don't say that," Callie said, tears forming. Her mascara was already ruined from crying earlier.

"You don't understand," Kody said. "Brett was aiming for me. It should have been me. Why did Winters have to be so stupid?"

Gene watched his friend struggle. He had never seen Kody cry, but he thought he might very soon.

A police officer made her way up to where they were sitting. "Everything okay?"

"Yes ma'am," Gene said. "He's the one Brett tried to shoot."

Kody got up and pushed past his friends to get out of the auditorium as fast as he could. Callie chased after him, while Gene continued talking with the officer.

"Kody, where are you going?"

"I need to go see Winters." When he walked outside, he stopped and looked around. "Crap."

"What's wrong?" Callie asked.

"I don't have a car."

"Car? You don't have a license!"

Kody shrugged his shoulders.

"Come on, I'll drive you," she said. "As long as I'm home before my dad has to work, it'll be fine."

Gene caught up with them as they walked towards the student parking lot. "Hey, where are you guys going?" he asked, slightly offended they appeared to have been just fine leaving without him.

"To the hospital," Kody replied. "Callie's going to drive. You want to go?"

Callie clenched her teeth and closed her eyes in frustration. Her friend truly was an adorable idiot.

"Wait, how can you drive?" Gene frowned, "You're not old enough yet."

And there it was. The question she knew was coming after Kody opened his mouth. Callie caught her breath. She knew Kody wouldn't question it. He would've just followed the trail of candy that led him into the car. Now that Gene was invited to go along, she would be forced to explain herself, and she didn't want to. If they found out the truth, they might stop hanging out with her. And she didn't want to lose their friendship. Especially Kody's.

"Well, you see," she began, slowly to give herself more time to think of something. "My dad forced me to learn," was all she came up with. Gene was sure to ask 'why'.

Thankfully, Kody's beautiful mind jumped in for the save. "Because he's a raging alcoholic?"

"Yes!" Callie said, relieved that between Kody's brain and mouth, there was a sieve. Even in this situation, the words just flowed out. It was a truth, however, which is what she wanted to tell. Kody had seen her father's alcoholism firsthand. There was more to her driving than that, but now wasn't the time to get into it. And her father being an abusive alcoholic was all she needed to distract Gene from wanting to know more. Gene was always seeking information. It was like his primary function in life was to absorb as much knowledge as possible.

It would be insensitive to pry further, even for Gene, she

realized. She silently thanked Kody.

The ride to the hospital was relatively quiet. With the condition of Dean Winters being in question, and Callie's dad being an alcoholic having been finally said out loud, there was an air of awkwardness. Nobody wanted to say anything out of place. Kody's mind kept replaying the moment when Dean Winters had gotten shot. He had come up with ten different ways he could have stopped it from happening. His mind raced as each scenario played out in his head. Even though he stared at the cars on the highway, all he saw was Dean Winters getting shot, over and over again.

Kody was in such a daze, he didn't realize they arrived at the hospital until Gene knocked on his window from the outside. When he looked up, they were in the parking garage and his two friends were waiting patiently outside of the car. He unbuckled himself and got out. Callie put a comforting arm around him as they walked inside.

At Port Haven Medical, the three friends were given stickers to wear as identification, then made their way up to the fifth floor where Dean Winters was resting.

As they approached his room, a nurse walked out. "Oh," he said. "You've come at a good time. He just woke up. Have you visited him already?"

"No," Callie said. "We're students at his school. We just wanted to see how he was doing."

"Awesome," he said. "Just to let you know he, like, literally just woke up. He can't say much yet, and what he can say is kind of hard to understand. He's going to have a long recovery."

"But he'll be okay?" Gene asked as he tried to peek into the room.

"For the most part, yeah," the young nurse replied. "He'll never walk again though. Bullet went right through his abdomen and into his spine. He's one lucky sonuvagun."

"Lucky?" They all said in unison.

"Well, yeah," the nurse replied. "Getting shot at close

range like that, missing all the vital organs. Can't believe he's alive, honestly." The nurse excused himself and went to the nurse's station.

"You okay?" Callie asked Kody, taking his hand.

A sense of calm washed over him. "Yeah," he said. "Let's go in."

When they entered the room and stepped around the privacy curtain and to Dean Winters' bed, they were taken aback. There were all kinds of machines hooked up to him, and tubes entering his wrists. He looked like he had aged thirty years.

Gene examined the monitors as he became fascinated with the machines designed to keep Dean Winters alive. The room was silent, except for the steady beeping on the heart monitor.

His eyes were open, and followed them as they moved to his bedside.

"Thank you." Kody said. Not knowing Kody's secret, Dean Winters had been willing to take a bullet for him. No matter how mean he seemed, or how critical he had been, this man was a hero.

Dean Winters nodded and whispered something Kody could not understand.

Callie put a hand on Kody's shoulder. "Mr. Winters, I just want to say I'm looking forward to having you back at school. I'm sure you'll be out of here in no time," she said. "Who else is going to yell at us to get to class?"

Gene's head poked up from behind one of the monitors. "I would venture to say everyone would welcome you back," he said. "Even Kody here."

"It's true," Kody nodded. "Who's going to write me up? Or constantly question my choices?" He chuckled nervously to try and fight back his tears. "I mean, I know you hated having me in detention with you, but there were easier ways to get out of doing it."

Dean Winters lips curved ever so slightly. It looked like he was attempting to smile, but since Kody wasn't sure the man knew how to, it was hard to assume.

But it was enough to let Kody know that things were going to be okay.

STEPHEN J MITCHELL

Gene asked to be dropped off at his house after they left the hospital. Dean Winters' condition intrigued him, and he wanted to get right home so he could start reading medical journals. If it were anyone else in the world, Callie and Kody would've questioned it, but it was pretty normal behavior for the little genius.

After dropping Gene off, Callie drove Kody to the dojo. As they drew near, she gasped, and pulled the car quickly over to the curb, ignoring the striped parking spaces.

The storefront had been vandalized. The front door had been forced open. The modest sign that read 'Tatakai Aikido' lay smashed on the ground.

Kody had known it would just a matter of time before

the ninjas came back to destroy the place. They had promised they would not stop, and now they had declared war.

"Kody." Callie's voice shook as fear took over her mind. She wasn't sure what else to say, but saying his name made her feel safe.

"Maybe you should stay in the car," he said. He didn't want her going inside. If the ninjas were waiting for him, she would be put in danger. As far as Callie would know, this was just a random break-in.

"We need to call the police." She reached out and grabbed his arm before he could get out of the car. "I'm not sitting out here by myself."

"From what I've seen, the cops here are pretty useless," Kody replied. He conceded that she wasn't about to sit outside alone, so he tried to downplay what may have happened, "Let's just take a look around first. Maybe it's not so bad. I'm sure Shihan handled whoever broke in."

The two of them got out of the car and stepped through the broken doorway. Kody insisted on going first to make sure the coast was clear.

The place looked like a bomb had gone off inside. There were gaping holes in the drywall and the front desk was in shambles.

"Shihan?"

He heard his grandfather groan from underneath some rubble and broken furniture. Kody frantically began clearing away everything he could move, as Callie stood over him, watching, hoping the old man who had raised Kody was okay.

When he was finally extricated, Shihan Toshihiro groaned feebly. "The briefcase."

"It's okay," Kody reassured him. "It's someplace safe."

"Briefcase? Kody, what's he talking about?" Callie asked.

"Nothing," he replied. "He's probably just delusional."

"Then why did you say it's someplace safe?"

"Just trying to keep him calm," he said. "We'll sort it out

later. Stay here with him and call an ambulance. I need to check the rest of the place out." He wondered how much damage they did searching for the briefcase, which he had hidden at Gene's house.

Kody made his way upstairs to the living space he shared with Shihan Toshihiro. His grandfather. That was still weird to him, and he wasn't sure if he should, or even wanted, to accept it. The man had raised him, so he definitely loved him. But, since he had been lied to his entire life, Kody wasn't sure if he could trust him. What else could he be hiding?

Upstairs, both doors to the loft had been broken. Frantically, Kody ran through his room and to the fire escape so he could get to the roof. He had stuffed his superhero costume in the utility room up there for safe keeping. If whoever had broken in went up to the roof, they may have found it. Bursting through the access door, he ran over to the small, brick, closet-like room and threw open the door.

Tucked away safely inside were his mask, trench coat, bandolier, and hoverboard. He hastily put everything on. With Callie occupied tending to Shihan and calling the ambulance, he could try to track down the ninjas and exact some revenge. Just as he put his arms through the sleeves of the trench coat, he heard a scream from the street below.

He ran to look over the side of the building just in time to see three men shoving Callie, kicking and screaming, into the back of their car—a car that had a dented hood and a cracked windshield. It was the same one that hit him before.

"I've got to stop them!" Kody said to himself.

Turning back to grab his hoverboard, he saw the short man dressed in the dark red ninja outfit and bandages on his face.

"I warned you," he said with his raspy voice.

"Where are they taking her?" Kody demanded through gritted teeth, his fists clenched.

"That's none of your concern, seeing as how you're

about to be...preoccupied." Bloodbath held his arms out, and ten other ninjas revealed themselves, pulling themselves up over the ledge and onto the roof.

"Look, Bloodbath," Kody warned. "In the last week, I've gotten into a fight at school, shot at, hit by a car, and I got detention. I am *not* in the mood for your shenanigans!"

"Simply surrender the briefcase, and you and your friends will be spared." Bloodbath held out his hand.

Kody yelled in protest. "I. Don't. *Have it!*"

"Then where is it?" The ninjas fanned out behind Bloodbath, each assuming a different fighting position, waiting to strike.

"Oh, I just remembered," Kody quipped. "It's up your butt and around the corner, ya pajama-wearing putz."

Kody charged, but Bloodbath was too quick. He side-stepped and slapped Kody on the back of the head. When Kody stopped himself and turned, he was surrounded by the ninjas in white.

He smiled. "Okay, well, what's a boss fight without a few adds?" Kody slid into a ready stance, his feet shoulder-width apart and his arms held out wide. "I just want to warn you guys, there's no respawning beyond this point. Make sure you save your game, or you'll have to start over when I'm done with you."

One-by-one they charged him. He used every bit of his training to weave through their attacks, using their incoming momentum to put them on the ground. Grabbing wrists and elbows as they attacked, he wasted very little energy. His aikido training rushed through his mind, and each attack was something new to focus on. It was as though the faster and more chaotic things were, the more his mind settled down.

As soon as one ninja would fall, another would come in with an attack. Kody shifted his stance, grabbed an arm, bent the elbow, and the attacker flipped head-over-heels in order to avoid a broken arm. After rolling to the ground, they would get up, dust themselves off, look for an opening, and attack again.

After the second round of futile attacks, Bloodbath shouted, "Enough!"

The men got up, some holding their backs, arms, or any other part hurt from being tossed like ragdolls.

"You are unable to defeat my ninjas," said Bloodbath. "And they are unable to defeat you. It would seem we are at an impasse."

"If by impasse you mean beating me is 'impassable,' then yes," Kody said with a smile.

"You are an idiot," Bloodbath said. "I'll be doing your girlfriend a favor by killing you."

"I don't think you're fully aware of - wait did you just call her my 'girlfriend?' First off, no, she's like, my best friend. Secondly, you have no idea what you are up against," Kody said confidently. He could take all the beatings Bloodbath could dish out. He was bulletproof, after all. Let him pull knives, Kody thought. They wouldn't hurt him one bit.

Bloodbath slid in quickly, delivering a two-fisted blow to Kody's chest, knocking him to the ground.

Kody stood up, inspected himself, and held out his arms. "See?" he said. "Didn't even hurt. And we've seen how ineffective your butter knives are."

Bloodbath moved quickly, again, and began pummeling him with a flurry of blows. Kody wasn't fast enough to stop any of them.

The next thing Kody knew, the bandaged man was behind him, locking an arm under his chin in a chokehold. The punches were just to throw him off guard!

Kody grabbed at the arm, his eyes wide. The grip tightened, and he struggled to breathe.

"First you will lose consciousness," Bloodbath hissed. "Then you will die. Some people prefer to die in their sleep. I guess I'm doing you a favor."

"A favor?" Kody gagged. He gasped for air. "I don't think you... understand what... being a... villain means."

"The more you talk, the harder it will be to breathe."

"Now... you're giving me... advice?" Kody struggled to pull Bloodbath's arm away, but the grip continued to tighten. He slapped at Bloodbath's arm, and his hand hit the bandolier across his chest. He heard a pulsating sound, followed by a rapid beeping. One loud buzz and a blinding flash of light later, a thunderous boom sent Bloodbath flying off of him.

The bandolier sparked.

Kody turned to look at his attacker, lying stiff on the ground, eyes wide open with shock. His men stared at their master, who twitched as sparks of electricity trickled around his body.

Kody inspected the bandolier. "Genius."

Ignoring the ninjas, he ran to the utility closet and grabbed his hoverboard and mask. Without wasting another moment, he slid his mask on while racing to the edge of the roof. He jumped over the side and tucked the hoverboard under his feet. The board hummed to life, and the thrusters kicked in as he skipped off the pavement and leaned forward.

Rocketing down the street, he hollered, "*Wa-hoo!*" The chase was on!

The HUD in his visor lit up green, and he gained night vision! "*Genius!*" He put his arms behind him and leaned forward further, reducing his drag and allowing him to shoot off into the night like a bullet.

"*Kody?*" Gene spoke to him. "*I just got a notification that the mask and hoverboard have been activated? What's going on?*"

"Genius! You are a genius!"

"*I could have told you that, but since you already knew it, I'd have been wasting both of our time. Which I've now done by explaining that.*" Gene sounded irritated. "*I repeat, what's going on?*"

"Remember those two guys that hit me with their car the other day?" Kody asked. "They just kidnapped Callie, and there's a third person with them now. They're working with Bloodbath!" He paused, then added, "I'm in pursuit!"

"*Give me one second.*" Gene began typing away on a keyboard. "*I accessed the traffic cams, and can track their movements from here. They're headed into the city.*"

"That's kind of what I figured," Kody replied. "Like, why would they go anywhere else?"

"*You'll want to go faster, though.*"

"And how do you suppose I do that?" he asked. "I've reduced my profile as much as possible to prevent drag."

"*Wow, it's almost like you paid attention during the 8th-grade bottle rocket unit,*" Gene said. "*Remember how I said there are switches near your feet? Slide your front foot forward and you'll get a boost.*"

Kody looked down at his feet and saw a red light. Following Gene's instructions, the board widened his base, allowing for additional balance--which he needed when the thrusters kicked in!

Kody already felt like he was moving faster than a bullet. Now he was hoverboarding on a missile!

"Alright bad guys," he said. "Buckle up, because I'm about to 'brake' your plans!"

"*That,*" Gene said, "*was awful.*"

STEPHEN J MITCHELL

Kody followed the beige sedan into the city. He wasn't entirely sure how he was going to stop the car; being bulletproof didn't exactly give him super-strength. If he tried to run them off the road, Callie might get hurt. But he also didn't want to risk following them into some secret hideout where hundreds of henchmen might be waiting to jump him.

He sped up to the driver's side window and knocked on it.

"Excuse me, sir," he said casually, as though they were not both speeding down the highway. "Would you mind pulling over so we can talk?"

The driver jerked the wheel, but quickly regained

control. "What the-!"

The passenger reached across the driver's face, pointing his gun at Kody. "Want me to empty my clip?"

"Get that thing out of my face, you moron!" The driver slapped the other man's hand. "Are you crazy? You're gonna get us all killed."

"Right," he said. "Roll your window down first. *Then* I'll pump him full of bullets!"

"Put your gun down. I'm just gonna run this freak off the road." The driver yanked the wheel toward Kody.

Kody was knocked backward. He bounced off another car and lost his balance. He hit the ground and rolled as the hoverboard careened away. Other cars swerved and honked their horns as they tried to avoid him.

He got up and took a moment to regain his senses. He survived it without harm to himself, but being a human pinball was disorientating. "Well," he said while inspecting a tear in his sleeve, "that was rude."

"*Kody, are you okay? The tracking beacon I installed on the hoverboard disappeared!*"

"Tracking beacon?" Kody replied. "Wasn't the board just supposed to be a cool birthday gift?"

"*I like to plan ahead.*"

"Of course you do." Kody waited for an opening in traffic and ran across the highway, where he picked up both pieces of the board. "It's a little broken." He jumped when one of the wires sparked.

"*Hold them together.*"

Kody held the pieces together and waited. "Nothing's happening," he said. "Should I just start running?"

"*Stand by please, I'm working.*"

The wires sparked again, and Kody held the board out away from his face, looking to the side. The wires then retracted into the board, and the two pieces snapped together.

"Whoa! How did you do that?" Kody exclaimed as he shook the board.

"I like to plan ahead, remember?"

"Yeah but how did you know it would break like that?"

"Well, for starters, I made it for you."

"Rude."

Kody ran and tossed the board out in front of him. Jumping on it, he immediately hit the boosters and began weaving in and out of traffic to catch up to the car.

He saw the car exit the highway up ahead, and he raced down the off-ramp when he got there. Gene provided him directions and offered a shortcut by slipping through some alleyways. That proved to be a little tricky as he dodged trash, hopped a fence, and avoided hitting a homeless person, but he finally got in front of the car.

He waved back at the driver.

"Now you can shoot him!" the driver yelled.

Leaning out the passenger window, the hefty man began firing shots. Each bullet thudded against Kody and bounced off, harmlessly. When the clip was empty, Kody shrugged an apology for his durability.

The car swerved around him and sped off. But when the driver tried to take a sharp turn down a side street, he lost control and crashed into a dumpster.

Callie emerged from the car a bit shaken, as she tried to escape and the three men quickly jumped out to pursue her.

Kody kicked off of his board, propelling himself into the air. At the apex of his leap, he saw the men standing over Callie. The short one, who had been hidden in the backseat, held a knife. Kody flipped the board into his hands and launched it at the knife. A loud crack echoed in the alleyway, and the attacker fell to the ground, clutching his mangled wrist.

Kody came down hard in a garbage bin.

"What was that noise?" Gene asked. *"Kody, are you okay?"*

Kody stood up and flicked some garbage off of his shoulder. "Yeah, I'm good," he replied. He hopped out of the dumpster and looked at the three men, whose focus was now on him.

"You think *you're* good? Think again pal," the hefty-sized henchman threatened. He aimed his handgun in Kody's direction.

"No, I was talking to…" Kody pointed to his ear. "You know what? Never mind. You gentlemen better scatter unless you want to end up like that dumpster."

"Oh yeah?" the driver replied. "*You* better scatter, or you're going to end up back *in* that dumpster." He pulled his gun as well and aimed it at Kody.

"I could provide you with a list of 'bullet points' on why that won't work."

In his headset, Kody heard Gene groan.

Both men pulled their triggers repeatedly, filling the alleyway with the sound of gunfire until their triggers produced nothing but a clicking sound. One bullet struck him in the forehead, knocking him to the ground. The impact left his ears ringing, but he could hear the muffled sound of Callie's scream. He winced and grabbed his chest.

Plucking out a bullet that had lodged in his bandolier, Kody stood up and flicked it back at them.

"You…you're *bulletproof?*" Callie said in shock.

"There's no way," said one of the men. He inspected his handgun. "I thought maybe his jacket was Kevlar or something, but I hit him in the square in the head. He should be dead!"

"The boss said these bullets were 'cop killers'," said the driver. "Kevlar can't stop them."

The third guy who had the knife finally stood up, still holding his wrist. After a quick consideration of what he had seen, he opted to run out of the alley.

Kody took a step toward the other two. They flinched. "Now, run along," Kody said. "And send Bloodbath a message. Tell him I said to take the next ship out of Port Haven, or I'll sink his entire operation."

"This is our turf!" the hefty guy replied. "If we don't walk it, we don't get paid. We're gonna get murdered if we don't report back in empty-handed."

Kody picked up his hoverboard and placed it on his back. "This isn't your turf," he said. "Not anymore. Maybe you should consider a career change because either your boss kills you or I beat you down. Sounds like a bad day at work either way."

"*What?*" Gene exclaimed. "*Don't threaten these people Kody. Are you crazy?*"

The two men ran out of the alley as sirens wailed in the distance.

"As unconventional as it was," Callie said, "thank you."

Kody stood with his back to her and looked over his shoulder. Even though he was wearing a mask, he still felt uncomfortable having her look straight at him. It was as though she could see right through his disguise.

Clearing his throat, he tried to lower his already synthesized voice. "You're welcome," he said. "You should probably get to the hospital to make sure you aren't injured from the crash."

"*Kody, you need to get out of there,*" Gene urged him. "*The police are almost on the scene.*"

"I think I'll be okay," Callie said. "But you…" She took a step towards him, and he quickly grabbed at his hoverboard and hopped on.

"Hey, Ge-" Kody caught himself before saying Gene's full name out loud, "-nee-us. Hey Genius, how do I get out of here?"

Callie cocked her head. "Are you asking me?"

Kody's face flushed red under his mask. "What? No!" he said, startled. "I, uhm, I gotta go. Take care of yourself. Maybe I'll see you around!" Leaning forward, he began to float toward the end of the alleyway.

Callie tried to follow. "Wait!" she called out to him. "Who are you? How did you do that"

"Isn't it obvious?" he called back over his shoulder. "*I'm bulletproof!*" And with that, he gave the board a kick and rocketed away.

"*You're pushing it with her,*" Gene warned him. "*She'll know who you are.*"

"I know," Kody replied. "Hey, help me get home, okay? I think I'm lost."

As Kody made his way back home, his hands kept touching the places where he'd been shot. There was something eerie about being invulnerable. He wondered if he would have been brave enough to do this if not for that.

Brave like the man who took a bullet for him.

As he weaved in and out of people who dared walk the streets at night, he thought that if he could keep Callie safe, why couldn't he do the same for everyone else? He may not have done much as boring old Kody Haywood, but anything was possible now that he was…

…bulletproof.

"You have a visitor."

The security guard unlocked the door to Brett Walker's cell. It wasn't exactly prison, as it was partially furnished, but it definitely wasn't home either.

Brett stood up and followed the white-haired guard out into the hallway. The guy was clearly too old to be a police officer, Brett thought. Probably just wasn't ready to retire yet. He hoped he would never be so desperate that watching over troubled teens was favored over greeting people at the local 'Good Buy'.

Although it did look like that's where the guard bought his uniform.

When Brett had appeared for his arraignment, the judge

was lenient on him. It seemed Brett's popularity extended even to the court system, as the judge had rambled on about how he was once a star athlete himself. He had seemed sympathetic to the pressures of balancing a social life, living in a broken home, and maintaining a high GPA, all while staying in shape and constantly preparing to win the next game.

Given that Dean Winters was still alive, Brett wasn't being tried for murder, but he had been sentenced for several counts of assault with a deadly weapon. Due to his lighter sentence, and considering his age, Brett had landed in Port Haven's Juvenile Correction Facility.

Also known as, 'The Chamber.'

The guard led him out into the common room, where several of his other 'roommates' were sitting at tables talking with visitors of their own. He clenched his fists and gritted his teeth when he saw who his visitor was.

Kody Haywood.

Brett tried to turn and leave, but the security guard stopped him with a surprisingly strong grip on his shoulder. They locked eyes with each other. The old man's gaze was cold and full of contempt, daring Brett to try breaking away.

Begrudgingly, Brett sat down.

He stared into Kody's eyes with a fiery intensity, trying to match that of the guards.

"Brett--" Kody began.

"Don't 'Brett' me," he spat. "You should be dead."

"Well, seeing as how you're emotionally dead, that would at least put us on some common ground," Kody teased.

"Screw you, I'm out of here." Brett moved to stand up, but the security guard pushed him back down. Brett looked up at him angrily, "I don't have to listen to this idiot."

"Sorry!" Kody put his hands up in defense. "I was just trying to lighten the mood; bad choice of words though. Just hear me out," Kody begged. "Please?"

The one-time All-American athlete for Bannerville High

School, now Juvenile Detention Resident 08-0175, sat silently in protest.

Kody took a breath. "I know I can be difficult to deal with," he said. "It's just how I cope with things. Sure, it gets under people's skin, but it's the only way I know how to be. I can't control it; I'm just...me. I can promise you this, though: no matter what happens going forward, I'm here for you. I'm going to visit you and get to know you better.

"I should have done it a long time ago," he continued. "And I realize my mistake now. I didn't know you were going through all that stuff you said in the hallway back at school." Kody shifted nervously in his seat. "We're not so different, you know?" he continued. "We could find common ground. Maybe even be friends."

Brett glared across the table, clearly now wanting to be anything remotely like friends.

"I'm not giving up on you," Kody persisted. "I believe there's a good person inside just eager to get back out there and show the world what you're really capable of."

A long silence passed between the two of them, as Brett processed Kody's words. All he could think about, though, was how Kody Haywood should be dead right now.

"Go to hell," he grumbled.

Kody nodded. "Well, alright," he said as he stood up. "If that's where you want to start, I'd say that's progress. Good first step. Hold onto that passion, my friend. We're going to see this through."

Brett bolted from his seat and lunged at Kody, but the security guard yanked him back down by the collar of his blue jumpsuit "I don't ever want to see you in here again!" he raged. "Or I'll find a blade, and I'll cut you open!"

"Good talk," Kody said as the guard dragged Brett away, struggling to get free. "Looking forward to see you next week!" He added as a second guard came to assist.

Later that night, Brett lay in his cell, still thinking about what Kody said. On the surface, his advice seemed like the right thing to do. If Kody wanted to be his friend and help him rehabilitate, then perhaps he should allow him to do just that.

Especially if it meant getting out of the Chamber sooner.

After all, how could he show the world what he's really capable of if he was stuck in the Chamber? How could he expose Kody as a fraud from behind bars? Kody constantly antagonized him, Brett thought. He didn't deserve to be applauded as someone who took down a school shooter. Kody wouldn't be looked at like a hero if he hadn't snapped.

Brett realized his mistake; his anger had given Kody an opportunity to be exactly what Kody always wanted to be: a hero. Meanwhile, Brett would be forgotten, his legacy at the school ruined forever.

Fury boiled over inside him, and Brett let loose with a guttural scream. He flipped his bed over, then grabbed the bed frame and smashed it into the wall, kicking at it, over and over again. Get it out now, he thought. Get it all out.

He grabbed the bars of his door in both hands and shook them back and forth, rattling the metal. His tantrum continued for several minutes, riling up several of his neighbors who yelled back at him. After a few minutes he tired himself out. His cell was destroyed. His knuckles were bloodied from punching the walls, and his elbows were bruised from throwing them into the bars.

He slumped to the ground, panting heavily as he caught his breath.

That was it, he thought. That was the last rage storm he would ever display. It felt good to let it all out. Now he could begin his plan to rehabilitate and get out of the Chamber early. He would be a saint. A model inmate. Whatever it took to fool everyone into thinking he was reformed.

And once he got his freedom back, he would get his revenge on Kody.

He would be smarter, because he had plenty of time to think of his next move. Part of being a quarterback, after all, was understanding the defense. Get them to jump off-side or expose their plan, pre-snap. He would do the same with

Kody. Find out what he's doing, expose him, and then cut him apart like a surgeon.

Kody Haywood wouldn't even see it coming.

Inside of a dark room, in an undisclosed location in Port Haven, the man Kody had named Bloodbath was down on one knee. He knelt in a pool of light from an overhead lamp that served to blind him to anything that might move in the darkness of the room.

His clothes had stopped smoking from his earlier electrocution, his ninjas having helped him up after sparks stopped popping from his body. He was tired, hurt, and lacked the strength to pursue the boy.

Since he had been summoned, he had to assume his henchmen had failed to kidnap the girl and kill the boy hero. He knew relying on other people would be his downfall. He also knew this boy should not be underestimated. Either the boy was extremely lucky, very resourceful, or both. The next time they met, he wouldn't play with his food.

A group of footsteps echoed in the darkness. His body tensed. There were few things on Earth that frightened him; his tensing was from preparation, not fear. He was ready for a fight. They may have taken his blades, but he knew many other ways to kill people. His body was a weapon, his blades were just fun accessories.

As a mercenary for hire, with a face never to be seen in public, blood money and the Internet were the key to his livelihood; everything he needed could be dropped off at his doorstep, paid for by the lives he had taken. The market was bullish for killers, especially in a lawless city like Port Haven. The gangs were growing stronger, the police force becoming more corrupt.

And now The Khan and his army of terrorists were slowly closing in.

All because of this stupid boy that he couldn't kill.

The footsteps stopped, leaving the room eerily quiet. He slowed his breathing to listen for any additional movement. If they tried anything, he would be ready.

"You failed me." A voice said.

"It won't happen again."

"You've always been very loyal… 'Bloodbath'."

"Don't call me that."

"Isn't that what the boy called you?"

"Yes." Curse that stupid kid. He preferred being nameless. It was easier to avoid attention. Now people would start repeating that name and associating it with his work. Fitting as it was, he did not want a name. People fear the unknown much more than the known.

"Well then, since he embarrassed you, it would seem he earned the right to put a name on you," The Khan said. "As the leader of a worldwide organization of terror, I can appreciate the desire to stay hidden. Anonymous. If someone hears of *me*, they should be fearful. *You* are just a mere mercenary. Who cares what people think of you?

Especially since you're synonymous with failure, something I do not take kindly to."

"I know this."

"I've been burned once before by the promises of an American," he said. "Your people seem to thrive off of lies and deception. It's dishonorable. And in my world, that's punishable by death."

"The boy had help."

"I don't want excuses!" he roared.

"I need to deal with him first."

"You need to do what you have been paid to do! I am a very powerful man, and I can make even you suffer."

Bloodbath did not look up, although for a moment, he wanted to. He heard The Khan shuffling about the room, accompanied by other footsteps, including a set of stilletos. The woman in white was here as well. The added noise in the pitch darkness made it very difficult for him to key in on where in the room The Khan had stood. He wanted to kill him now but he would have go through everyone in the room and he lacked the strength to do it. And he had a soft spot for the woman in white.

She was the one who recruited him. Her little contest was to choose another champion. His replacement.

He wasn't above killing them all. But The Khan was wealthy, and he paid very well. Keeping him alive was preferable to finding other work. But if it came down to his life or The Khan's, he wouldn't think twice about how many he would have to cut down to escape. Except for her.

"I won't fail you again," he promised.

"I have no reason to believe you will," The Khan said warmly. "This is just a mere boy, after all, and my scientists tell me I don't need him alive to extract what I need. You've faced him in combat. You know what to expect now. I don't care who has to die, or who has to suffer. I want what is rightfully mine!"

The voice pierced Bloodbath's ears. He winced in pain as the acoustics of the room created a deafening echo.

"You will have his corpse," Bloodbath promised. "And the head of anyone who dares stand in my way."

"Good. Then our business here is concluded."

The Khan and his men shuffled out of the room, and the blinding light that shone down from the ceiling shut off. Bloodbath continued to kneel in the darkness. He would have to feel his way out of the room, back the way he had come. Fortunately, he was familiar with the path. He had been here before, when The Khan had given him his first contract.

Doctor Eric Haywood.

Haywood wasn't the first man he had been paid to murder, but tracking him down had certainly been the most fun. He didn't go down without a fight, but he was hardly the most difficult kill he'd ever had; it was well worth the money when it was over. But when The Khan had realized the formula he sought wasn't anywhere to be found, he grew angry. He was obsessed, and would stop at nothing to get it.

Now that they had located Haywood's son, The Khan believed the formula was still intact. Having faced him in person, it was clear to Bloodbath that whatever the good doctor had created had obviously been injected into the boy. He may have to alter the deal a little. Perhaps on top of the bounty, he would demand The Khan share this formula with him. It might have some healing properties and, with any luck, he could rid himself of the grotesque bandages perpetually wrapped around his face.

He smiled, and a sore cracked open. He pulled another patch of gauze from his pocket and stuck it to the seeping wound. Feeling his way to the exit, he stepped out into the hallway. He stared up at the two guards, both of their heads wrapped in cloth.

He sneered at them. "What the hell are you looking at?"

They looked at each other and smirked. "I'm not sure," one responded. "But it looks like a little pile of pig vomit."

Bloodbath made short work of them. He wasn't in the mood to play around, so after shattering one's kneecap and crushing the other's throat, he snapped the first one's neck and let the other suffocate from his collapsed esophagus. It was cleaner than he preferred. To do the job properly, he would first need to collect his blades, and he had no desire to come back to carve them up.

No, his efforts required focus elsewhere. A team of ninjas and a few local thugs had not been enough to take down that obnoxious brat. How was it the boy could be better trained than his own men?

As he thought upon it for a moment he realized it was the old man at the Aikido school. It just took him a while to realize it. For the recognition to set in.

Kaito Toshihiro, a once powerful figure among the *Himitsu no Senshi* in Japan. Kaito had fled to this country to protect his daughter, a daughter who was now locked away by The Khan.

Perhaps now she might prove valuable in another way. It was fortunate The Khan had chosen to preserve her.

As he collected his weapons from the security detail, he frowned at the guard who couldn't make eye contact. His grotesque appearance was his calling card. It made people afraid. One-by-one, he placed each of his blades back in their respective sheaths, attached strategically to his outfit: one on each forearm, two on each leg, four on his belt, one on each side of the bandolier that strapped over each shoulder, and one full-length katana on his back. Before returning the katana, he turned the blade over and stared at his own reflection. He would not fail again.

He needed to figure out how to kill this bulletproof child. And if the boy couldn't be killed, then Kaito Toshihiro would be the consolation prize. *Himitsu no Senshi* would be very pleased to have the deserter. And the boy might care enough about the old man to turn himself in to The Khan in exchange for his life. There was also the matter of the girl he had rescued; clearly, he had a soft spot for her as well.

The boy would most likely be on high alert, so she

wouldn't be as easy of a target right now, especially with her father's gang connections.

Everything started to come together in his mind, the threads of his plot slowly weaving together to form an intricate web.

He smiled. He knew what to do and this time there would be nothing the boy, could do about it. His target all along should not have been the child. He only needed to tip over one domino for the rest to fall in line. As much as he enjoyed killing for money, this job required more finesse and less stabbing.

Putting the sword away, he left the compound to put his new plan into action.

"I really appreciate you two coming over to help clean up the place," Kody said, tossing a large plastic bag of busted up debris into the dumpster in back of the dojo.

"You know I'm always here for you, Ko."

Kody's ears perked up.

"Why did you call me that?"

"I don't know," said Callie. "It just sounded right." She tossed an armful of junk into the dumpster and wiped sweat off her forehead.

Kody took a deep breath. "Callie," he said, faltering. "I need to tell you something."

Gene was in the dojo, gathering up more trash. Kody was not sure if this was the right thing to do, but he chalked it up to just being open and honest—which, to his mind, was always the right thing. Even if sometimes it bothered people to hear the truth.

Callie smiled and took a bottle of water from an ice-filled cooler set by the back door. "You can tell me anything," she said. "You know that." She twisted the top off the bottle and took a long drink.

"I'm bulletproof."

Callie choked, the water in her mouth spraying everywhere. "You're what? That's the most ridiculous thing I've ever heard."

"No, seriously," Kody said. "I'm bulletproof."

"How do you even know who that is?" Callie said raising an eyebrow.

"Who…?" Kody stammered. "Wait, are we talking about the same thing? I'm bulletproof. Like, I'm indestructible."

"Kody—"

"Callie," he said, cutting her off. "Gene knows. Shihan, I mean, my grandfather, he knows too."

Callie stared at him, jaw agape in disbelief.

"Watch," he said. He reached into the dumpster and pulled out a short piece of broken lumber with nails jutting out of it. Then slammed it into his own abdomen, and the nails popped out the other side of the board.

"*¡Dios mio!*" Callie exclaimed. She lifted his shirt to see if he was hurt. "Not a scratch," she murmured, brushing her fingertips across the place where the nails had hit. She looked up at him, and her face went flush as she realized her hand was on his abs. She quickly pulled it away and took a step back. "So, it was you I pulled from the water at the pier?"

"Callie, yes, that's what I'm trying to tell you," he said. "And what were you even doing out there anyhow?"

"I was waiting for my dad to get out of… work," she replied. "He had business at the docks. And now I guess you know his dirty secret." Her shoulders slumped. "I'm so embarrassed."

Kody shook his head. "Don't be," he said. "Everyone has their demons. Maybe we can get your dad some help."

"He won't want it," she replied. "This is how he chooses to be. I can't wait to get out of his house."

Kody sighed. "I wanted to tell you about my secret sooner, but I was scared," he said. "Now I wonder, if I *had* told you, maybe you'd have been better prepared when those 'ninjamas in pajamas' showed up to distract me while the goons kidnapped you."

Callie smiled weakly. "It doesn't surprise me," she said. "You've always been *my* hero. Now you just have powers to go along with it."

Kody let out a short laugh. "Wait," he said. "You really thought my name was Bulletproof?"

"Well you were all like,"—she lowered her voice— "'*I'm bulletproof*,' so I figured that's what you meant."

"Hah! No, that was just me letting you know they couldn't hurt me."

"Well, it's not a bad name, you know."

"No," Kody agreed, mulling it over. "I guess it's not."

Gene came out and tossed some drywall into the dumpster, then reached for a bottle of water from the cooler. "What are you two talking about?"

"I told her I'm bulletproof."

Gene dropped the bottle. "You did what?"

Callie laughed. "I'm guessing if he's Bulletproof, that means you're the Genius?" She picked up the dropped bottle and handed it back to him, "Because your name is Gene, and you're really smart. Clever. So, do I get a codename?"

"This is getting out of hand," Gene said.

"What?" Kody protested. "She has a right to know, especially since she's already been dragged into it."

"That's fair." Gene relented, taking a drink of his water.

"So, what's my codename going to be?" Callie asked.

"I don't know. Code names just kind of happen, I guess," Kody said. "But I'm sure we'll come up with one.

Usually it depends on your set of skills. How about, *El Companero?*"

Callie shook her head. "No, I don't think so. I'm nobody's sidekick. But clearly, you've been studying for your Spanish final, so that's good to know," she teased.

Kody shrugged and smiled.

The three of them walked back inside tossing around potential codenames for Callie. As they talked, Kody looked around at the dojo, ripped to shreds. Plaster had been pulled from the walls. The desk had been destroyed. Even the practice mats were torn up and overturned. His grandfather had deemed the place unsalvageable.

Kody watched as the old man sat on the sidewalk outside the front door, dabbing sweat off his forehead with a dirty cloth.

Callie walked up to Kody and put a hand on his shoulder. "You should go talk to him."

"Yeah," Gene said, dragging a broken chair towards the back for the large rusty dumpster, which was already half-full. "Callie and I can take over for a bit."

"I know what's on his mind," Kody said. "The man just lost the only thing he had left in life. This dojo was it for him. He used it to raise me after my mom—"

Callie put an arm around him. "Hey, we're here for you, right?" she said. "No matter what happens. Whether you re-build or just move somewhere else, Gene and I will always have your back."

"Where have I heard that before?" Kody shot a glance at Gene, who innocently pushed the broken chair out of the dojo and began whistling nervously.

"Seriously, go talk to him." Callie nudged him forward. "I'll be in here if you need me."

Kody watched as his friend began sorting through more of the damage. Looking over at his grandfather, he wasn't sure what to say.

As he approached, the old man wasted no time.

"Sit," he instructed. He patted the ground next to him.

Kody did as he was told. There was Grandpa Toshihiro and Shihan Toshihiro and right now, he was sure who he was about to talk to.

It felt like an eternity passed before he finally mustered up the courage to ask the big question.

"So, what happens now?"

Shihan looked upward, wistfully. "Maybe I'll open an all-you-can-eat buffet."

Kody smiled. It made him happy to hear the old man make light of the situation. "I'm surprised to hear you cracking jokes," he said. "This is pretty serious."

"If there is one thing I have learned from you," his grandfather replied, "it is that I cannot take things too seriously."

"Gene would be the first to tell you that you never have to worry about me being too serious."

Shihan smiled and continued. "You have a way about you that allows you to just enjoy the moment, without being bothered by things you cannot control." Shihan Toshihiro put his arm around Kody and patted him on the back. "You are very Zen."

Kody smiled back. "Well, I do have a suggestion grandfather," he said, then paused. "Can I call you that now? It feels weird."

"I would like that, yes," Shihan replied.

"What if," Kody said, "instead of a blatantly obvious Japanese buffet or Aikido school, we go with something a bit more subtle. Something that doesn't scream, 'Old Japanese dude inside!' Like, maybe, a pizza place?"

"A pizza...*place*?" His grandfather's face twisted as though he just bitten into a sour grape.

"Yeah," Kody replied. "Pizza. Look, there are very few things in life that make me happier than comic books and video games. Pizza is one of those things. And I want it to be a place where people feel safe to just come in and chill." He looked back inside at Callie. "You know," he said, "someplace where people can escape their problems at home, school, whatever."

"A safe haven for today's youth." Shihan mused. "But not one that will make us stick out like a sore thumb to these ninjas that have taken an interest in you and I."

"Exactly!" Kody exclaimed. "You've busted your butt and risked so much to take care of me. Let me do it for you now." Kody drew himself up with authority. "And," he added, "we can donate a portion of the profits to a foundation for mental health awareness." He immediately thought about Brett.

"*¡Muy bien!* I think that's a wonderful idea!" Callie cried as she wrapped her arms around Kody from behind.

"Yes," Gene added, following Callie outside. "That's very admirable of you."

Shihan Toshihiro sounded a bit more skeptical. "It is," he agreed. "But I don't know if the insurance money will cover such a business venture."

"You just let me handle that," Kody replied. "I'm sure I can figure something out. I'm pretty resourceful you know." He looked at Gene, who nodded back at him.

"Well then," Shihan said, as he stood up. "It looks like I have more to learn from you than I thought."

Kody clapped his hands together in celebration. "And the student becomes the master!" He pumped his fist in the air.

Shihan Toshihiro handed Kody a broom. "The student also becomes the janitor," he said.

They all laughed and went back to picking up the pieces. Kody couldn't think of a better way to start his next chapter.

Kody climbed up onto the ledge of his building, sat down, and dangled his feet over the side. Sitting alone in the dark allowed him some time to think. He had a lot of questions that needed to be answered, and he didn't have a clue where to begin looking.

It would be much easier if his father just showed up mysteriously and started explaining things to him.

"Is this your new hangout?"

Startled, Kody swung his feet around and stood up, ready to defend himself.

The masked man in gray was on his roof.

"What are you doing here?"

"We can help each other," Gray replied, ignoring the

question.

"Help each other? How?"

"I need to protect my interests. My employer—"

"The Khan," Kody interrupted.

Still ignoring him, Gray continued. "He desperately wants what you have," he said. "You've clearly already been exposed to the serum, and it's working; which means you probably have questions that need answering."

"Serum?"

"Oops! I've said too much." Gray said in a dry, mocking tone. "Yes, serum. It's what made you indestructible. The research was stolen by your father. And not only the research, but the laundered money from my employer."

"Just say The Khan," Kody said, exasperated. "Why won't anyone just say it?"

Gray's face betrayed no hint of emotion. "I've decided it may be better to offer you something in return for your father's research."

"Like?" Kody asked.

"Your mother."

Kody's eyes widened. "You know my mother?"

"Yes. Her name is Sue."

"Where is she? Is she okay? Does she know anything about me?" Kody got goosebumps hearing someone else say his mother's name. Then a chilling thought occurred to him. "Wait...are *you* my father?"

At that Gray cracked a smile under his mask. "Ha! Not a chance," he said. "And if you think I'm going to sit here and be interrogated by you, you're wrong. Like I said, we can help each other. I know where she's being held. But I can't walk away empty-handed, or my life is forfeit."

"Is Bloodbath after you, too?"

"He'll stop at nothing, and destroy everything," Gray said flatly. "Which is why you have to cooperate with me. My employer,"

"The Khan," Kody corrected, again.

"He has enlisted many people to come after you, but I

just can't go through with it. I have a soft spot for you boy."

"Man, you're annoying. Is that your superpower?"

"No. But I'm very perceptive," Gray replied. "And I know you'll be compelled to find your mother now that you know she's alive."

Kody took a moment to process his thoughts. "How can I trust you?" he asked. "How do I know that you aren't going to double-cross me? You abandoned me at the harbor and left me for dead. You're letting people hold my mother hostage instead of saving her. You're practically a villain but it's like you're not sure yet."

"Me?" Gray replied, eyebrows raised in offense. "You almost got your Dean and a classmate killed. Sounds like you're the one we should be worried about."

"How did you know about that?"

"I'm very perceptive," Gray said. "I literally just told you that."

"Yeah, but...ah, never mind," Kody said. "I probably wasn't paying attention. My brain doesn't work like it should."

"Think of the lives we could save working together," Gray continued. "Why should you be the only one with this gift? What if we could make people resistant to diseases that destroy cells? Cancer would be a thing of the past. Not even The Meteor is indestructible. Imagine not having to sacrifice lives to win wars anymore. We could remove dictators from power, and liberate enslaved nations without casualty."

"I'm no honors student," Kody said. "But I think you can do that with diplomacy."

"Talking never works!" Gray barked.

"And yet," Kody shrugged, "here we are."

Gray's expression became dark. "Do not test my patience, Kody," he said grimly. "I have very little time to play games."

Kody walked up to Gray and looked up at the taller man, defiantly. "I've got all the time in the world, and no reason to trust you."

Gray reached up to his mask. "Not everything is as it seems," he said. He looked down and pulled off his mask. A scar ran over his milky white, right eye, and extended down to his strong, chiseled jaw. Aside from that, his face was nearly perfect. Combined with his dimpled cheeks and blonde hair, the man was a work of art.

"My name," he said, "is Nate Powell. I was your father's lab partner."

ACKNOWLEDGEMENTS:

I would like to thank everyone who has put up with listening to me talk about this character over the years. I can't wait to share more of his adventures with you.

ABOUT THE AUTHOR

Stephen J. Mitchell grew up on cartoons and comic books during the greatest decade of pop-culture known to mankind. Born and raised in upstate New York, he went on to raise three children of his own in the suburbs of Syracuse. A lover of nature, he enjoys camping, hiking, and kayaking; his greatest achievement, however, was his trek up Mt. Marcy, the highest peak in New York State.

After writing countless articles for blogs and pop-culture websites, he won an award for his short story in an anthology published to raise proceeds for a charity. Combining his passion for kids, pop-culture, and adventure, he is now focused on writing novels for a new generation of readers who live in a fast-paced world seeking instant gratification.